THE GRIM JOKER

Reynaldo Reyes had a reputation as a man who liked a joke. A bad joke.

Now the butchering bandito had Skye Fargo, the girl Antonia and the half-mad trooper Barney at his mercy. Killing them would be easy. Too easy for Reyes' twisted taste.

Smiling, he tossed Fargo's unloaded gun back to him. "I am a kind man," Reyes said. "I will leave you three bullets. One for each of you—when the desert becomes too unbearable."

Fargo stood with the trembling girl and the shattered soldier and watched Reyes and his men ride off laughing. He looked at the three bullets lying in the sand, and felt the sun already turning his throat dry as dust.

But the Trailsman felt another thirst as well—a thirst to see those bullets and have the last laugh. . . .

THE
SILVER
MARIA

by

Jon Sharpe

A SIGNET BOOK

SIGNET
Published by the Penguin Group
Penguin Books USA Inc., 375 Hudson Street,
New York, New York 10014, U.S.A.
Penguin Books Ltd, 27 Wrights Lane,
London W8 5TZ, England
Penguin Books Australia Ltd, Ringwood,
Victoria, Australia
Penguin Books Canada Ltd, 10 Alcorn Avenue,
Toronto, Ontario, Canada M4V 3B2
Penguin Books (N.Z.) Ltd, 182-190 Wairau Road,
Auckland 10, New Zealand

Penguin Books Ltd, Registered Offices:
Harmondsworth, Middlesex, England

First published by Signet,
an imprint of New American Library,
a division of Penguin Books USA Inc.

First Printing, September, 1992
10 9 8 7 6 5 4 3 2 1

The first chapter of this book originally appeared in *Snake River Butcher*,
the one hundred twenty-eighth volume in this series.

 REGISTERED TRADEMARK—MARCA REGISTRADA

Printed in the United States of America

The Trailsman

Beginnings . . . they bend the tree and they mark the man. Skye Fargo was born when he was eighteen. Terror was his midwife, vengeance his first cry. Killing spawned Skye Fargo, ruthless, cold-blooded murder. Out of the acrid smoke of gunpowder still hanging in the air, he rose, cried out a promise never forgotten.

The Trailsman they began to call him all across the West: searcher, scout, hunter, the man who could see where others only looked, his skills for hire but not his soul, the man who lived each day to the fullest, yet trailed each tomorrow. Skye Fargo, the Trailsman, the seeker who could take the wildness of a land and the wanting of a woman and make them his own.

New Mexico Territory, 1860,
a simmering desert
where men will stake their lives,
betray their friends, and sell their souls
to find the lost legend of the Silver Maria . . .

1

"Tell me where it is. Now."

He heard the words through the roaring in his ears and he willed the muscles of his tired neck to shake his head.

"Never," he heard himself say, as if from a distance. The warm blood was dripping down his neck. He felt the searing pain where his ears had been torn and sliced from his head. Soon it wouldn't matter. The man had already killed Barney and thrown his body into the pit. Soon he would kill him, too. How long? Time had no meaning here under the blazing sun, his blood running down his neck. But he would bear any pain.

He looked up into the face of the man. He had never trusted him. How could he have been so stupid not to see what was coming? And where were the others? The others he had trusted and led for many years? The man had ordered them to tie him spreadeagle to a boulder. Then they left, not looking back at him. Not wanting to know what would happen.

"Then I will get the information out of Antonia," the man hissed. "Yes, that will be a pleasure."

He felt the breath leave his body and pain, pain he could not bear, clutched his chest.

"Antonia knows nothing," he said. *"Nada."*

The man struck his face with all his force and he felt his head bounce painfully against the boulder.

"Don't speak that Spanish shit to me! Tell me. Where is the Silver Maria?"

He hesitated as the man drew his knife and took a step forward. He looked up into the man's face and saw there the curse that had killed men and made men kill other men for over three hundred years. He saw lust for blood, for silver, in the other man's face. And he smiled. He couldn't help himself. A tight smile, a grimace of pain, of recognition.

The man screamed with rage and lunged forward, knife upraised, grasping his hair with one hand. He closed his eyes tight, straining against the ropes and felt the excruciating heat of the knife piercing his eyelid, entering his eye, twisting, rough-cutting his eye out of the socket. Throbbing blackness welled up around him and he heard from a distance, "Tell me. Where. Now. Or Antonia dies. Or worse."

The words were wrenched out of him and he tasted his blood in his mouth. "Mission . . . Ascension. Padre . . . Ernesto." He felt the void of despair after the words were spoken. "Just . . . leave Antonia . . . alone."

"She's a pretty little snot," the man said, tightening the grip on his scalp. "Too pretty to be left alone."

Then, far away, he felt the man grasp his scalp again. More pain, but duller, his other eye cut out, the heat pouring down his face and an odd coolness on his forehead, a lightness, like floating. Then a fumbling, his arms and legs being cut free of the ropes and falling, landing on something soft. Barney, he thought. His loyal friend. And with the last of his remaining strength, he contracted his muscles, embracing the man who lay under him at the bottom of the sand pit. He felt Barney stir.

He realized he would bleed to death, here at the bottom of this pit in the desert heat, his eyes cut out of their sockets, his ears sliced off. Send Antonia help, he said in his mind. But who could help her when the curse of the Silver Maria corrupted all men? And suddenly, the picture of a tall silent man riding alone came into his mind. Maybe there was a hope. Then, above, he heard the click of a hammer. Gunfire. And nothing.

Fargo was a silent shadow, a slowly moving blacker blackness in the night as he slid silently along the side of the cabin, careful that his boots did not crackle the dry gravel and that he did not brush against the creaky board wall. He paused and listened. His acute hearing picked up no sounds from inside the flimsy shack. All was still.

He waited, muscles tense, his Colt revolver glinting faintly in the pale starlight. Far off, he heard the low whistle of a screech owl and the nearer rustle of night wind over the low sage. As he rounded the corner of the building the moonlight struck him. He glanced up at the new moon hanging newly risen above the horizon against the pale starlit sky. It was nearly midnight. Where the hell was she?

Fargo edged closer to the cabin door, a tall muscular man, wary, coiled as tight as a spring, his face in shadow. Then he heard it. Inside. The barest dry rustle. A slight scurrying, the whisper of a movement. He tensed and moved to the door.

With a swift motion he kicked open the door and jumped aside. There was silence inside. He regarded the black gaping doorway.

"Antonia?" he said to the darkness. No answer.

He removed his hat and tossed it across the threshold. It fell inside onto the floor.

Fargo relaxed and smiled to himself. Nothing in there with a gun, he decided. He pulled the tinder box from his pocket and struck a light, holding the flame in front of him as he ducked his head into the shack and leaned down to retrieve his hat. The light lasted long enough for him to see a rusted iron bedstead, a table, and several broken chairs. A movement, a sideways scrambling on the floor, caught his eye as the light flickered and failed. He heard the dry rustle again. He backed out and pulled the door shut behind him. Scorpions, he thought. And he reminded himself to shake out his boots before putting them on in the morning.

Skye Fargo slowly scanned the terrain in front of the shack, noting the arrangement of rocks and sage. He walked quietly to a tall outcropping nearby, and climbed up several feet, bracing himself in a narrow cleft, hidden in shadow. He looked down over the solitary cabin and the trail which led to it in the dim moonlight. To the west he saw the stark rock walls and the opening to Loyal Gulch. That was the landmark. The message said to meet her at the cabin at the mouth of Loyal Gulch. At midnight. Now where was she?

A few minutes later, Fargo heard his pinto nicker. The Ovaro, tethered out of sight in the sage, smelled something approaching. The nicker was a warning, but the pinto would not make a noise if anything strange was within earshot. Hoofbeats sounded, coming fast. Fargo cocked the Colt and waited.

On the trail he saw a lone horseman, riding hellbent, a flicker of movement on the dark sage plain. The rider galloped up the trail and pulled up short before the cabin, swinging down to dismount, with a swirl of riding cape.

"Skye?"

Fargo relaxed at the sound of her voice, but did not move. He watched as she looked about nervously. She tethered the horse to the hitching post by the door of the shack.

"Skye?" she called again. Louder this time. He heard a trace of nervousness in her voice.

"*Mierda!*" she cursed in Spanish, stamping her foot impatiently. Fargo smiled to himself and watched as she paced back and forth a few times. And he listened. He listened to the silence of the trail behind her. Was she being followed? But the night stayed quiet.

Fifteen minutes passed while she paced before the cabin, patting the neck of her horse from time to time. The message from her said her life was in danger. That usually meant somebody was hard on your heels. If somebody was following her, they weren't close behind. It was time to let her know he was here.

"Antonia," he said and saw her jump. She took a stumbling step toward her horse, as if to mount. "I'm here. It's Skye Fargo." At the sound of his name she turned and peered into the darkness toward the rock outcropping.

"Skye? *Valgame Dios!* Why didn't you answer me? Where are you?"

He was beside her in a moment.

"Antonia," he said as he hugged her close, noticing her soft yielding curves under his hands. "I wanted to be sure you weren't being followed. Well, well. Antonia Delgado. It's been many many years." He held her at arm's length. "My how you've grown."

He had last seen her as a young girl with blazing black eyes, gawky and shy as a newborn fawn. But now before him stood a full-blown woman, her ebony hair streaming long behind her in the night wind. The riding cape and wide skirt hid the curves he had em-

13

braced. He took her chin in his hand and turned her face toward the pale moonlight. It was a beautiful face, the jet eyebrows arched and glistening above two eyes so fiery black that they glittered even in the near darkness. Her eyes hadn't changed. Her full lips smiled.

"Skye Fargo," she said in a low, rich voice. "Thank you for coming to help me. You are a true friend . . ."

"That's me," he said.

"And a friend of my father." He heard her voice catch on the last word.

"Yes," Fargo answered. "Yes. Friend of your father. Rest his soul. And Julio Delgado was a friend to me. When I needed him once, he saved my life."

"Well, now I need you," she said.

"Come with me," Skye said. He took Antonia by the hand and helped her up to his perch in the cleft in the rock. "From here, we can watch the road behind you. Just to be sure. Your message said your life's in danger. I don't want anybody jumping us while you tell me what's up."

She settled herself between two rocks and Fargo's lake blue eyes quickly scanned the nubby sage plain. No movement.

"What's going on?" he asked, directing his full attention to Antonia.

"I . . . I don't know," she said.

"You told me Julio was killed."

"*Sí. Sí.*" She spit the words, bitter words, and Fargo saw tears of sorrow and rage glisten in her dark eyes. She held up her hand, as much to halt him from answering as to stop her tears. "Crying will not bring him back," she said. "My father was a hero. He truly lived every moment of his life, holding nothing back. I will not cry. It does him dishonor." Fargo watched as she bit her lower lip and regained control.

Watching her, he thought of Colonel Julio Delgado, as he had last seen him years ago, waving goodbye, sitting high on his mount in his U.S. Army uniform. Delgado had been a legendary fighter in the war with Mexico and had been rewarded with the command post at Fort Managa.

The command hadn't been an easy one. Fort Managa was a lonely outpost, Fargo remembered. After the war, there were many years of constant trouble with Mexican raids across the border. And recently, the Apache had been tricked by unscrupulous settlers and treaties and had become even more ferocious.

But Colonel Julio Delgado had been equal to all this and more. In Julio's veins ran the mixed blood of Spanish nobility, Mexican grit, Indian cunning, and white ambition. He had been a man that other men would follow, tireless, selfless, brave. A man who rode in front of his men into battle. A man who never asked his men to do what he would not.

Julio Delgado had saved his life once, risking his own to free him from the Apaches. It had been a long time ago. And now, Julio Delgado was dead.

"How did it happen?" Fargo asked.

"I don't know," she answered. "Father sent me to New Orleans. He told me to get some new dresses and supplies. But actually, I think he wanted me to be away from our hacienda for a while. Something was going on that he wasn't telling me."

"How did you know that?"

"One night I surprised him and Barney McCann in his study. They were looking over an old document on his desk. I had come in with the coffeepot so quietly that they didn't hear me until I was next to the desk. When Father looked up and saw me, he jumped and hid the document. The next day he sent me to New Orleans."

15

Fargo remembered Barney McCann, Julio's sergeant. A rotund man with an infectious laugh. McCann was devoted to his commander.

"And then?"

"That was three weeks ago that father sent me away. A week ago, while I was still there, I received the message from Padre Ernesto."

"Which said?"

"I have it here." She reached inside her cape and drew out a folded letter, handing it to Skye. He unfolded the paper and held it so that the moonlight fell across the page. He could barely make out the heavy strokes of the quill pen.

"My Spanish isn't great at night," he said, handing it back to her. She read it to him quickly:

"Your father has been murdered. Your life may be in danger. He has left you something. Meet me at the cabin at the mouth of Loyal Gulch. Trust no one. Signed, Padre Ernesto."

"That's everything you told me in your letter," Fargo said. "This Padre Ernesto is a man of few words. Is he trustworthy?"

"Completely," Antonia said. "I have known him all of my life. But of course, I was worried. I thought if I was in danger, it would be good to have someone along."

"Someone you could trust," Fargo said. She nodded slowly. "So you sent me a message." She opened her mouth to answer and Fargo heard the Ovaro whinny, low. He put his finger to her lips and looked out over the sage.

Far off he saw a bobbing movement, the slow progress of a lone rider wending his way up the trail toward Loyal Gulch. Fargo drew the Colt and watched. Why was he riding so slowly? Was he wounded? The figure was wide and bulky. As the mount drew near, Fargo saw that there were two riders on one mule and in the same instant, before he could stop her, Antonia jumped down from the rock outcropping and ran toward them.

"Padre! *Gracias a Dios*!"

"Antonia!"

Fargo looked across the plains again as he lowered himself down. There was nothing moving in sight.

The monk had dismounted and stood beside the mule. He was a stout man, muscular under his rough woven robe which was belted with a piece of rope. His bald pate shone like a polished egg in the pale moonlight.

Antonia was kneeling and kissing his hand. On the mule sat another figure, a large man, his hat brim pulled down low over his face and the collar of his jacket up around his neck. Fargo could not see his face in the shadows, but the man sat motionless, looking straight in front of him as if unaware of where he was.

Antonia got to her feet as Fargo approached.

"Padre Ernesto. This is Skye Fargo."

Fargo touched the brim of his hat.

"Skye Fargo," the padre repeated in his heavy accent, rolling the *R*. He peered at him in the gloom. "That name has traveled a long way. It has crossed the dry devil lands and come to the heart of the country, to the little Mission Ascension where I live. And the name of Skye Fargo has many legends attached. Almost as many as the lost Virgin Maria!"

"I asked Skye to meet us here," Antonia explained. "He was an old friend of my father's."

The padre crossed himself.

"May he rest in peace," he said. "If half the legends of Señor Fargo are true, he is the kind of man who can help you in your trouble."

"But what is my trouble? And how did my father die?" Fargo saw her brace herself for the answer. She was courageous. She was Julio's daughter.

"Your trouble is very grave, my child," the padre answered her. "Your father was found in the desert at the bottom of a pit which had been constructed so that he could not climb out." He paused as if to find the words for what he had to say next. "He had been tortured." Fargo heard Antonia gasp. The padre turned and put his hand on the arm of the man sitting silently on the mule. The man shifted and obediently dismounted with the padre's help. Then he stood as if waiting to be told what to do.

"This man was found with your father in the pit," the padre said gently. He removed the man's hat. The top of the head was bandaged heavily. Beneath the bandages, the face was swollen, the eyes small and dark and completely blank.

"Barney!" Antonia moved forward as if to embrace the man. Barney took a step backward, raising his arms as if to ward off a blow. Antonia paused. "Barney. It's me. Antonia. Antonia Delgado."

McCann began to gasp as if he could not breathe. He fell to the ground and twitched, then lay still, moaning and gasping, his hands groping in front of him. Antonia knelt beside Barney, placing one of her hands on his shoulder as he lay on the ground. She bent down her head as if praying over him. The padre moved away and Fargo followed.

"This man was in Delgado's regiment. A sergeant," he said to Fargo.

"I know Barney McCann."

"This is not Barney McCann," the priest said. "Barney McCann no longer exists. His mind is completely gone."

"Who did this?" Fargo asked.

"I think it must be Reynaldo Reyes," the priest answered.

Fargo nodded. He had heard of Reyes and his gang of *bandidos*. They had terrorized New Mexico Territory for a decade, stealing horses, rustling cattle and holding up the stagecoaches. So far, the Reyes gang had eluded capture. They knew the territory and could appear and disappear in those winding canyons like cloud shadows on a windy day.

And Reynaldo Reyes. The very name terrified the settlers in the remote haciendas along the border settlements, especially those with womenfolk. Reyes had an appetite for women, Fargo had heard, an insatiable appetite. And he was wily and greedy, often adding some last act of ironic humor to his most dastardly deeds. The Reyes gang was interested in two things—money and women. But torturing two men in a sand pit in the desert?

"Somehow, this doesn't sound like Reyes to me," Fargo said thoughtfully. "Torture isn't his style."

"Reyes is *el diablo*—the devil himself!" said the monk. "*Sí*. Mark my words. It is Reyes."

"Where was Julio's regiment when he ran into . . . Reyes or whoever? Why were he and Barney traveling alone?"

"That I do not know," the padre answered. "The regiment, maybe they were chasing Apaches. It was bad luck for Julio not to have his men around him in his moment of greatest need."

"Agreed," Fargo said.

"A great man," Padre Ernesto said. "And such a crime to lose such a one by the hand of this *bandido* Reyes! He and his gang have made the trouble for the heart of the country for many, many years. And no one can catch him."

"The heart of the country?" Fargo repeated, keeping his doubts about Reyes's involvement to himself. "You said that before. What does it mean?"

"The heart of the country is the land where I live, the area surrounding the Mission Ascension," the padre explained. "It is said that the Virgin Maria herself is hidden there in the hills. For three hundred years, she has been the heart of the country and watches over us. You have never been there?"

"No," Fargo answered. "I was in the western side of the territory when I met up with Julio Delgado and Antonia. She was just a girl then."

"She is still a girl in many ways," Padre Ernesto said, turning to look at Antonia, who was still kneeling beside Barney McCann. "You must look after her, Señor Fargo. I hope you can be trusted. She needs such a friend as you."

"I owe Julio a debt," Fargo said. "Looking after Antonia is a small repayment."

"It is good to repay old debts," the padre said. "It keeps the heart pure. But now, I must do what I came to do."

The priest walked to the mule and removed a flat wooden box from one of the saddlebags. Antonia lifted her head at his movement. Barney McCann was lying still on the ground.

"Come, my child," Padre Ernesto said, helping her up. "Two weeks ago, your father came to me and gave me this box. He made me promise that I would deliver this box to you if anything should happen to him. He said that it is a letter to you. We will take it inside and you can read it there in peace."

Fargo stepped forward with his tinderbox.

"Stay here," he said, lighting one of the candles the priest handed him and going inside. The flame made his shadow loom large on the rough walls of the shack. He held the candle low and examined the floor. There it was under the iron bedstead. Fargo moved softly across the floor and stamped on the scorpion. He continued to look about. They were always in pairs. Nothing on the floor. He held the candle high and looked at the walls and ceiling. Nothing.

Fargo turned, called them inside, and then spotted the mate clinging to the doorjamb, tail raised, ready to strike. Antonia entered, placing her hand just below the scorpion, and with one swift step Fargo was beside her, brushing it off the doorjamb. The scorpion landed on the floor. Fargo gave it a kick with his boot and it slid across the floor, then scuttled away quickly, disappearing into a floorboard crack.

"Escorpion!" Antonia said with a shudder.

"Two of them," Fargo said, gesturing.

"It is bad luck to kill only one scorpion," she said. "Very bad luck."

"But good to be merciful," the priest said. He set the wooden box down on the table. He drew a thin chain up from inside his robe and lifted it over his head. On it was a small key which he handed to Antonia.

"Padre Ernesto, how can I thank you?"

"This is not necessary, my child. We will leave you in peace to read the letter from your father."

Fargo left the shack with the padre. Barney McCann still lay where they had left him.

The priest motioned him to walk away from the cabin and from Barney. When they were just out of earshot, the priest turned to Fargo and looked him full in the face.

"I hope you are a truly trustworthy man, Señor Fargo," he said.

Fargo shrugged. "More than most," he said.

"Because Antonia needs someone to help her. She is in terrible danger."

"Because of what is in the box?" Fargo asked.

"Perhaps."

"Do you know what is inside?"

"I only know what Julio told me. He said there was a letter inside for Antonia. Please take the box to her, he told me. You see, Señor Fargo, a priest must be the guardian of many secrets. This is true in the confessional. I know too many secrets already which weigh upon me. So, I did not look inside the box. I do not want to know any more secrets. It is enough that I have delivered this box to Antonia."

Fargo nodded.

"But you think she is in danger. Why?"

"As soon as we found Julio and Barney McCann, I sent the message to Antonia. I left as soon as supplies could be packed on my mule. While I was on the way here, I received word from Mission Ascension. An hour after I left, three masked men came to the mission. They were looking for the box of Julio Delgado."

Fargo whistled softly. "Probably the men who murdered Julio. They must have tortured Julio and Barney to find out where it was. You were lucky to have left before they arrived."

"Yes. Luck, or God's will. I am sure it was Reyes and his gang," the priest said. "Anyway, these men asked where was the box of Julio Delgado. Well, my brothers are not stupid. They said it is not here. They said one of our brothers went on a mule with it to California. My brothers could only think of this story to tell, part of a lie, to send them in the wrong direction. They could have made a better lie if they had more time or if they were better practiced at telling tales."

"So the masked men took the trail toward California looking for a priest on a mule," Fargo said.

"Exactly," said Padre Ernesto. "But . . ."

"But, how long did it take them to realize that they were going the wrong way? That they should have caught up with a priest on a slow mule already?"

"*Sí*. It would not be hard to find the trail of a priest on a mule," said Padre Ernesto.

"They are not far behind you," Fargo said, looking thoughtfully out at the sage plain again. "Does Antonia know any of this?"

"No," the padre said. "She has been very brave about the death of her father. But I do not want to add to her burdens."

"It is better not to tell her," Fargo said. "You didn't tell her much about how Julio died either. That was good."

"What would be the point of her knowing how much he suffered?"

"Exactly," said Fargo. "But I'd like to know what you found. Maybe you can tell me something that will shed some light on this."

"It was the most horrible sight I have ever seen," Padre Ernesto said, rubbing his forehead with one hand. "Our little Brother Saludo came across them. He just happened to be following a stray lamb into a blind canyon and he came across the sand pit. He hurried to the mission and many of us came back to help get them out." The priest hung his head as if unwilling to say more. Fargo waited.

"There they were," he continued, "at the bottom of this pit of death, under the blazing sun. At first, we thought both of them were dead. Around the top of the pit were ropes and blood. We think that Reyes had been torturing them for a while and then lowering them back down into the pit. For several days at least. We raised the body of Julio first. His eyes had been gouged out and the ears cut off his head. He had been beaten very badly too. Only a devil could do this."

"Or several devils," said Fargo.

"At first, we thought Barney McCann was dead. He lay under Julio. He had been shot in the head and his blood was all over him. But when we raised him up, we found he had not been mutilated and the shot had not killed him."

"So, they shot Barney and threw him into the pit first," Fargo said. "Interesting. They thought they had killed him."

"Yes," Padre Ernesto said. "But why didn't they torture Barney as they had Julio?"

"They were trying to find out something. That's the usual reason for torture. They were trying to find out the location of the box. And something or someone, probably Julio, convinced them that Barney didn't know anything. If I ever knew Julio, he tried to convince them that Barney was useless to them, hoping to save him. But instead of letting Barney go, they shot him and focused their attention on getting the information out of Julio."

"*Sí.* That must be how it was," the priest said softly. "But then, eventually, he told them. He told them that the box was with us at the mission."

"Yes, every man has a breaking point."

"But Julio Delgado?" said the priest. "He was a man made of the very rock of the country!"

"They threatened him with something. Something worse than death."

The priest looked at Fargo questioningly. Fargo nodded toward the shack where Antonia was. The priest nodded.

"Yes. In my heart I know this is the truth," the padre said.

"What's interesting is that Julio knew he was in danger. He sent Antonia away three weeks before, out of harm's way. A week later he left the box with you. A week after that he was found dead in the sand pit. I wonder if he knew who was after him? I wonder if he wrote it into the letter to his daughter?"

They both looked at the shack, golden lit in the darkness. Julio had died thinking he had saved his daughter, Fargo thought. He had died thinking she was safe in New Orleans, even if the torturers got the box. But who would have guessed that the padre would have set out so quickly. And would have actually delivered the box to Antonia. Now she was in danger. They all were.

"What you have told me tonight," Padre Ernesto said, "shows me that you can read the lives of other men. This is wisdom. I can rest easier knowing that Antonia Delgado will be with you, Señor Fargo," the priest said, patting his arm. "If there is any path out of her troubles, you will be the one to help her find it."

"I will try," said Fargo. They turned back toward Barney.

"I think he would feel better if he walked a little," Padre Ernesto said, helping Barney to his feet. "It has been a long, uncomfortable ride."

"Don't go far," Fargo said.

"No one is more aware of the danger of Reynaldo Reyes than I," the monk answered. Fargo climbed up the rock outcropping again and watched the priest and Barney walk back and forth in front of the cabin.

The landscape was silent and still, the trail cutting dim curves through the sage. The golden candlelight seeped between the warped boards of the shack. The wan light of the new moon, now high in the sky, illuminated the steep walls of Loyal Gulch, turning the jagged rocks into weird forms and faces. The rotten terrain, riddled with caves, was ideal for mountain

25

lions, Fargo thought. It was time to bring the pinto out of the sage and closer to them.

As he rounded the back of the cabin and passed by the window, Fargo glanced in. Antonia Delgado stood at the table, in profile. In one hand, she held a candle. With the other, she held a document up at eye level. Even at the distance of ten feet and through the dirty windowpane, Fargo could see that the document was old and that it had drawing on it. Like a map. But what caught his attention was not that. It was the look on Antonia's face. On her face, that beautiful face, was a confused mixture of utter disbelief and abject terror.

2

Fargo paused and watched as Antonia continued to examine the map, her eyes darting wildly across the page. Then he heard the padre's footsteps on the other side of the cabin, approaching the door, and the sound of his knocking.

Antonia jumped at the sound, almost dropping the candle.

"Just a moment," he heard her call and watched as she hastily folded the document, unbuttoned her blouse, and thrust it inside.

Fargo moved on toward the Ovaro. He thought of Antonia surprising Julio and Barney McCann in the study. The document—the old one Antonia had described on Julio's desk—was clearly the same one as she had held in her hand. But what was on that map that would make Julio—and now Antonia—so jumpy and secretive? What would she want to hide even from Padre Ernesto? Fargo was certain that the map had caused Julio's death. But how? And who? And how close were they to Antonia?

The pinto was glad to see him and stamped impatiently.

"Hey," Fargo said softly, stroking its muzzle as he untethered the Ovaro. He led it down to the trickle of creek and let it drink long. He let his mind wander as he watched the pony graze, admiring its muscled shoulders and haunches and its alertness. The Ovaro's unusual markings—black with a pure gleaming white midsection—made it look, in the deep blackness of the gulch, like two halves of a horse, front and rear, with the middle missing. Fargo smiled at his own fancy.

Pintos were prized for their hardiness, intelligence, and loyalty. This one had more of those qualities than any other pony Fargo had ever owned, ridden, or seen.

The two of them, horse and man, had been on the trail together for a long time. How many times had the pinto saved his life? It had outrun Indians, outlaws, and stampeding buffalo. Signaled him when it smelled danger approaching. Moved with complete silence through dark nights of vigilance, tracking, seeking, finding. And on long rides, the pinto went on when all other horses had fallen to their knees and refused to budge.

Fargo felt a surge of gratitude and affection for the horse and he stroked the rippling muscles of its shoulder while it nuzzled his chest. He clucked his tongue softly and moved toward the cabin. The Ovaro followed. There wasn't another horse like that anywhere, Fargo thought.

He picketed it by Antonia's roan and the padre's mule. Antonio heard his movement and opened the door. The yellow candlelight made a glow around her.

"Where's the padre and Barney?" Fargo asked. He would not let her know what he had seen inadvertently through the window. If she wanted to tell him about the map, she would.

"They've bedded down over there beyond that rock," Antonia said softly. "There is something else about Barney. He would not come into the shack with the padre. He is afraid of closed rooms now. Because of his . . . experience." She shuddered and Fargo knew she was thinking of the horrors Julio had faced in the sand pit.

"You afraid?" he asked as she drew her shawl around her shoulders.

"No. No. I am not afraid," she said. But something in her voice said that she wasn't sure of her answer.

"What is it then? Something in the box?" She looked at him as if measuring him.

"Yes, Skye. It is . . . it is a burden that was in the box. Yes, a burden that I have." Fargo thought of the map and the way she had hidden it from the padre.

"Anything you want to talk about?"

She looked at him for a moment and then looked away, as if afraid to see what was there in his face.

"I cannot," she said. "I can share with no one. It is a secret, a secret that has killed and might kill again. I must find the way. I must find what to do with it." Antonia shook her head from side to side as if saying no to some voice inside of her.

"I'm here if you change your mind," he said. "I'll help you if I can. For Julio's sake. All you have to do is ask me."

"I know that," she said. "Perhaps the time will come when I feel I can ask you. But I must have some time to think it over. Yes. Then I will know what to do next."

She tossed her head, a defiant gesture, her long dark hair cascading over one shoulder.

"You remind me of Julio," Fargo said.

"Everyone always said that."

"I never met your mother," Fargo mused as he gazed at her, the golden light outlining her strong, clear features. "She must have been very beautiful."

Antonia's dark eyes shone. Behind her, Fargo could see the iron bedstead, with her trail blankets spread out on it. She followed his gaze and then her eyes returned to his.

"I never met my mother either," she said. He started to speak, but she cut him off. "Tonight I am very lonely," she said, taking a step toward him. "I will tell you something now. It has been a long ride to this meeting at Loyal Gulch. Every hoofbeat of the way, I have been torn in two. I have been torn between my grief and my . . . You see, when I was not thinking of my father, I was thinking of you."

She paused, her eyes searching his. He smiled down at her and took her hand in his.

"When I was a girl," she said, "and you came to visit my father, I idolized you. I always . . ."

"Hush," he said, laying his finger on her lips. He stepped closer to her and bent over her as her face came up to meet his, lips parted, eager. Her mouth was sweet, her hair smelled of cinnamon. He explored her with his tongue and his hands, enjoying her softness and fullness. Then he stepped back from the doorway.

Antonia's eyes blazed hurt.

"What? I thought that . . . after all these years. Maybe you think I am still the little girl? Is that it?"

"Oh no," said Fargo with a grin. "I'd like to come in. Really I would."

"Then you are teasing me."

"No. It's just that I don't know this area, Loyal Gulch, real well. And I don't trust it." He didn't want to tell her about the three masked men who were following the padre, trying to get Julio's box.

Antonia looked worried.

"Do you think we should stay here for the night?" Fargo shrugged.

"It's too late to move on now. Besides, this is an easy place to keep an eye on. And that's what I intend to do. All night. From up there." He nodded his head toward the rock outcropping.

"I understand. *Gracias*, Skye," she said softly, and she reached up to clasp her hands behind his neck to bring his mouth to hers again. This time, she held nothing back, exploring him as he had her, and he drank in her sweetness until his head reeled.

"Whoa," he said, stepping back. "Another time, Antonia."

"Promise?" she said, her eyes full of black fire.

"No promises necessary between old friends," he answered her. "Another time, at the first opportunity." She smiled.

"Buenas noches," she said, closing the door behind her.

Fargo turned reluctantly away, still feeling her warm mouth on his, her taste still on his tongue. He climbed again onto the rock outcropping and braced himself in the crevice. He turned his collar up against the night air and leaned back against the cold stone. The golden light was extinguished in the shack. A soft snore came from where the padre and Barney McCann were sleeping. The horses snorted in their sleep from time to time in front of the shack. The new moon climbed higher in the sky and then descended toward the west. A mountain lion yowled once in the distance, but didn't venture near.

The distant sage plain and the winding trail remained empty. Still. And this was what Fargo watched through the night.

Padre Ernesto was up before dawn. Fargo descended from the rocks when he saw him making his way to the creek to wash up.

"You have not slept, Señor Fargo?"

"I wanted to keep watch," Fargo said.

The priest nodded.

"Antonia is blessed by such a loyal friend as you," he said. "Get some sleep and I will keep watch on the road for the next few hours. I have my prayers to say and I can look out at the same time. God will understand."

By the time the padre had returned from the creek, Fargo had laid his bedroll by the rock outcropping which would shade him from the morning sun. The priest dutifully climbed up to the lookout point and Fargo fell onto his bed, grateful for rest.

Sometime later, in midmorning when the sun glared on the canyon walls above, the sound of their voices awoke him. They were speaking softly, but the rocks reflected their low voices down to him.

In his half-sleep state, he could make out some of the Spanish words. Antonia was giving confession to the padre. This could be interesting, he thought, turning over in his bedroll so that he could hear better. He had never heard a confession before. She said his name and then the words *pecado* and *lujuria*—sin and lust. Fargo smiled to himself. Then he heard the padre chuckle and she laughed as well. The sound of their quiet laughter brought him fully awake. What kind of confession was that? Then her voice became somber and it was harder to hear her. After a few sentences, her voice stopped abruptly and there was a long pause. A short question from the padre.

"No, no, no," Antonia said, and Fargo heard a note of sad resignation in her voice.

"*Gracias*, Padre Ernesto." Fargo heard her scrambling down from the outcropping and walking back to the shack. From their words he guessed she had come close to telling the priest about the map. But something had stopped her at the last moment. Fear. It was fear. But of what? Of whom? He turned over and went back to sleep.

The smell of warm tortillas and coffee woke him. The high noon sun blazed overhead. He stretched and rose, returned his bedroll to the saddle, washed up at the creek, and joined the group at the campfire.

"*Buenas dias*, Señor Fargo," the priest said as he sat down.

"How was the shack? Sleep well?" Fargo greeted Antonia.

"No scorpion tails in there," she said, winking at him. Fargo glanced at the padre who was looking down at his tortilla, unable to suppress the small smile on his round face.

The large form of Barney McCann sat on a rock, but instead of staring straight ahead, as he had done the day before, his gaze followed Antonia as she moved about serving the food.

"Eat this, Barney," she said gently as she handed him a plate and a tin cup.

"Ta weh," Barney said, looking up into her face.

Padre Ernesto started.

"He spoke! This is the first time he has said any word since we have found him!"

Barney quickly looked away from Antonia and down at his plate and his mug as if he heard but did not understand the priest's words.

"Barney?" Padre Ernesto said. "Barney McCann? Can you answer me?"

Barney continued to look down, then raised the cup to his mouth as if he did not know they were there.

"Is he deaf?" Fargo said.

"No," the priest said. "He jumps at loud sounds, so his hearing is not damaged. But he does not respond to our words."

Antonia approached him and laid a hand on his arm.

"Barney?" she said. The big man looked up at the sound of her voice and two tears rolled down his cheek. "Can you answer me?" she asked gently.

"Natonee," he said.

"*Sí*, Antonia," she answered. "Tell me, Barney." She paused for a long moment. "Who did this to you? Who killed my father?"

Barney's eyes focused over her shoulder and slowly widened in his swollen face, as if he saw something dreadful standing just behind her. Antonia looked about, but there was nothing there and she turned back to watch Barney. He began to stiffen and then to shake convulsively. He slumped over and rolled onto the ground where he lay still.

"It is too soon," the priest said. "Perhaps, with time, he will recover." He shook his head sadly.

"Is Antonia the only one he's spoken to?" Fargo asked.

"Yes," the padre answered. "The brothers in the mission tried when he was brought in. I tried on the way here. But he would say nothing."

"I would like to help him," said Antonia, looking down at Barney on the ground. "He was my father's best sergeant. And one of his most loyal men. I am sure Barney McCann would have died in my father's place if he could have. That was the kind of man he was. Now I will take care of Barney, Padre."

"If you are sure you want this responsibility," the priest said. Antonia nodded.

"Someday he may tell you who murdered Julio," Fargo said.

"Perhaps," the priest said. "But meanwhile, where will you go, my child? Back home?" Fargo heard the note of concern in the priest's voice. If the masked men got word that Antonia had the box, they might ambush her on the trail. Or wait for her at the hacienda.

"I do not know where to go next," she said. "I do not know what to do. I must have time to think and to plan."

"You are still troubled, my child," the priest said. "And it is a solitary trouble." Fargo thought of the incomplete confession she had made.

"Yes, Padre," she said. "I will know when the time is right to speak. I will know when to go. And where. But the time is not now."

"Sounds just like Julio," Fargo said.

"Let us speak of something else," Antonia said. "Tell me, Padre, is the little Mission Ascension still as beautiful as ever?"

"Like Eden on earth," the Padre answered. Fargo heard a note of sadness in his voice which Antonia did not appear to perceive.

"The amber stream still runs through the white-washed compound?" she said, her words rushing on when the priest nodded. "And the cottonwoods are there? The children of the orphanage still play in the shade?" The priest continued to nod as her voice grew dreamy with remembrance. "And every spring there are many new lambs. And the chapel? Still with the blue glass windows?"

"*Sí,*" said Padre Ernesto. "All looks as you remember it, my child." The priest's face fell. "But there is trouble even in Eden."

"Trouble? What kind of trouble could come to Mission Ascension?" Antonia said.

"Last year, a wealthy rancher discovered an old deed which showed that he owned the land under the mission and the orphanage," Padre Ernesto explained. "Even the fields where we grow our food to feed the monks and the children, he owns! And he is a greedy man."

"But what can this rancher do? He cannot take away the mission and the orphanage," she said.

"But, my child, he is. He has told us that he will close the mission, unless we can pay him the twenty thousand dollars to buy the land and pay him rent for all the years we have used it. And it is all legal."

"But that is robbery! And the children?" she said, her voice choking.

"He does not care for children," the priest answered bitterly. "He only cares for gold. And the children will be turned out. No homes. I do not know what we will do. The heart of the country is a beautiful land, but it is very poor. We cannot find twenty thousand dollars so easily. May the lost Maria save us!" The padre crossed himself.

Fargo watched as Antonia's face underwent a change. A light came into it, a kind of quiet fire, as if some great heat blazed within her.

"Do not lose hope, Padre," she said quietly. "Perhaps there is a way."

"It will be a miracle from God, then," the priest answered sadly. "Because we must have the money to pay him by the next new moon. That is only one month away."

Antonia looked thoughtful. "It is possible," she said, as if to herself. "Yes, it is just possible."

"Then I will pray for this possibility," the priest said, rising. "And I will pray for you too, Antonia Delgado. Now, I have done what Julio Delgado has asked. And I must be going."

"Now? So soon?" Antonia asked.

"Wouldn't you rather wait for us?" Fargo said, thinking of the three masked men. "We could ride out together. Where are you headed anyway?"

"I must journey to the Mission San Patricio now. Like you, Antonia, I know this is the time I must go."

"I'd feel better if we set out together," Fargo protested.

The priest waved his hand and he walked toward his mule.

"We are on different paths," Padre Ernesto said, untethering and mounting the mule. Antonia stepped forward and kissed the padre's hand.

"Go with God," he said to her. "And you," he said to Fargo. "Go with whatever it is inside which drives you onward. For you do not ride the ways that are known to many men." Fargo nodded.

"Keep an eye out, Padre," he said.

"I hope we will meet again under better circumstances," the priest said. *"Adios."*

They watched the slow progress of the mule across the sage plain until it was a small moving dot swallowed by the distance.

"What now?" Fargo asked her.

"I do not know," she said.

"Look, Antonia," he said. "It would help if I knew what was going on here. I'm happy to help you. But I can't if you're not telling me everything."

"Skye, I'm sorry, but the less you know, the safer you will be."

"Antonia, I won't push you. But I want to help."

"Please, Skye, trust me." She massaged her temples with her fingertips. "Give me some time to think."

"Sure," he said. "We're okay here, at least for the time being."

Fargo kept an eye on the trail while he watched her pace up and down beside the fire, then by the shack, her head low. Barney McCann, who had seated himself again on the rock, watched her all the while. Fargo started to call out to her once, to offer once again to help her if she would just confide in him. But it was useless, he decided, and stopped himself. She was a woman who would make up her own mind. It took only an hour. Then she suddenly whirled and came over to stand beside Fargo.

"I know now what I must do," she said. "I have decided. We must ride now. Quickly. And I need you to come with me."

"Where to?" Fargo asked.

"To the heart of the country," she said.

"Why?"

"I will tell you that," she said, her eyes suddenly laughing, "at the first opportunity." Fargo remembered his words to her the night before when he had refused to come inside the cabin.

"Promise?" Fargo said, smiling.

"No promises necessary between old friends," she answered.

They quickly put out the fire, refilled the canteens and packed the gear, saddled the horses, and mounted. They would start out with Barney riding behind Antonia on her sturdy roan. Later, they would trade off and Barney would ride with Fargo.

They galloped down the dry trail away from the mouth of Loyal Gulch, across the wide sage plain bordered by low canyon walls. They had only gone three miles when Skye's sharp eyes saw the dust and the glitter of a few dozen men riding toward them in the distance.

Fargo's thoughts flickered lightning fast. Reynaldo Reyes and his *bandidos*? Maybe. Maybe not. If Reyes and his gang caught them on the open trail, it would be rough going, particularly on Antonia. They could turn around and try to outrun the riders, but with Barney and Antonia on one horse, they would be overtaken in a few miles.

There was a chance they hadn't been spotted yet. Fargo pulled up and motioned to Antonia and they wheeled off the trail and headed for cover among some rocks at the foot of the canyon walls a half-mile away.

They were too late. Fargo looked over his shoulder and saw the riders had angled off the trail and headed across the open sage to intersect them. They would beat the riders to the rocks with a few minutes to spare. He looked back again, but the riders were too far away to identify.

The ground was a blur beneath him. He thought suddenly of Padre Ernesto. Whoever these riders were, they would have run smack into Padre Ernesto traveling alone on a mule. Fargo cursed himself for not insisting that the priest wait to travel with them.

Fargo tapped the Ovaro on the neck and it galloped even faster, drawing away from Antonia and Barney. He needed every second to find a protected spot for the three of them. The rocks came rushing toward them and he pulled up, jumped down and sighted a cleft, protected from the back. He could hold out there for a while.

He slapped the Ovaro on the rump and watched it run a short distance away. The horse would be safer out on the plains than in the middle of a gunfight. It would come back later to him when he called. Antonia and Barney arrived and he motioned them up to the cleft. He had just finished checking the loaded chambers of his Colt when the riders came close enough for him to recognize them.

He breathed a sigh of relief and holstered his gun.

"That's a welcome sight," he said to Antonia as he turned toward her. But Barney's face drew his attention. His blank eyes had widened and the shaking began again. Antonia put her hand out toward McCann, but he shrank back and continued to stare wild-eyed past Fargo at the plains. Fargo turned and looked behind him, but all he saw was Julio Delgado's U.S. Army Regiment in full uniform riding toward them.

3

"What is it, Barney?" Antonia asked the quaking man. Barney McCann covered his face with his hands and sank to his knees. Antonia looked across him to Fargo. "It's the regiment," she said, her voice lowered to a whisper, as if she were thinking to herself. "He's afraid of his own regiment."

"So it seems," Fargo answered her. He watched as the riders drew nearer, their U.S. Army-issued blue uniforms bright with brass buttons. "Something about them reminds him of the sand pit . . ."

"Is it possible that . . ." Antonia began, her voice tight with disbelief.

"Anything's possible," Fargo said grimly. "Stay here with Barney behind this rock. I'll see what I can find out."

"I'm coming with you," Antonia protested. "These were my father's men. I've known most of them all of my life." Fargo nodded and helped her down from the rocks. They walked out to meet them.

The troop rode in two double columns. An Indian scout galloped alongside on an Appaloosa, wearing the colored fabric headband and flowing mane of the Tonto Apache. The troop's leader was a tall man riding at the head of the column. He seemed to draw himself up straighter than necessary in the saddle. The flaring cuffs of his yellow kidskin gloves covered his lower arms and his black boots sported gleaming silver spurs. He reined in before them.

"Dismount!" he called with a brisk snap in his voice. Creaking and clattering, the troop swung out of their saddles, all but him. He continued to sit on his horse, looking down at Fargo and Antonia.

"Antonia Delgado!" he exclaimed. "We never expected to run into you. What are you doing in these parts?" Fargo noted the familiarity in the man's greeting, but there was something else he heard too. Something he didn't like. The man dismounted and stepped toward them.

"Fox Stalling," Antonia said, a cool distance in her voice. So that was it. There was some kind of history between these two. She stepped back, refusing to give her hand to the major. "Meet Skye Fargo."

"Skye Fargo?" Major Stalling said, suspiciously. "I know that name. You're called the Trailsman, right?"

"That's me," Fargo said.

"I am Major Fox Stalling," he said, repeating his name unnecessarily. "Posted to Fort Managa one year ago. Now commander of this troop." Fargo noted the bright gold stripes on the major's epaulets. There was no dust on them. Fargo wondered how often the major brushed them. Hourly? He smiled at the thought.

Fargo touched the brim of his hat to the major, who ignored him and turned back to Antonia. He swept the wide hat off his head and the hot sun glanced off his bright red hair and florid face.

"I was concerned about you when I heard about . . . about your father's death," Fox Stalling said.

"Murder, you mean," Antonia said. Fargo looked about at the rest of the troop. The men stood beside their sweating horses, listening, but with their eyes averted. Fargo recognized a few of their faces from years before and wondered if they remembered him.

"Colonel Delgado's death was most unfortunate," the major said.

Antonia ignored Stalling and looked over at the men.

"Hello, Brent. Justin. Bill Carmichael," she called out. Her clear voice cut through the air. The men shifted uncomfortably and avoided her gaze. "Hello, Joe Strayhorn," she said. A young man with bright blond hair looked up from the ground and ducked his head, then blushed and lowered his gaze again. They were certainly acting strange for men who had known Antonia Delgado all their lives. Not one of them greeted her. Not one of them said anything about the loss of their colonel, her father.

Major Stalling cleared his throat loudly. "Like I said, it's a real surprise running into you. I thought you were in New Orleans."

Antonia looked startled.

"Who told you that?" she asked.

The question seemed to take Fox Stalling aback and he glanced at Fargo furtively before he answered.

"Why, your father told me. Yes, Colonel Delgado told me." Fargo noticed that Antonia's hand was quaking slightly.

"When?" she shot out. "When did my father tell you I went to New Orleans?"

"Why, Antonia," Major Stalling said quietly, soothingly. "Colonel Delgado told me the day after you left. Before he . . . disappeared."

Antonia shook her head.

"He told no one," she said. "He told no one where I had gone." Fargo saw her trembling, as if suppressing a great rage or fear. She knew something, but what? Whatever it was, she might lose control any moment, Fargo thought.

"You're pretty far from Fort Managa," Fargo cut in to distract Stalling and give her a moment to collect herself. "What are you doing up north?"

Major Stalling took the bait.

"Two reasons. The goddamn Apache savages are acting up again. But the main reason is Reynaldo Reyes," he answered. "We're chasing him and his gang of bandits. It's dangerous work. Man's work. Not like breaking trails." Fox Stalling could get under a man's skin real fast.

"I've heard of Reyes," Fargo said nonchalantly.

"The Reyes gang has been terrorizing every stage-coach and traveler between here and the border. Especially the womenfolk," Major Stalling said. He spit on the ground. "He's had free rein in this territory for ten years. Now that I'm leading this troop, we're going to run down the Reyes gang once and for all."

Fargo ignored the subtle insult to Julio Delgado. But Antonia didn't. She turned pale with fury, spun on her heels, and walked over to her roan, a short distance away. Stalling's eyes followed her.

"Might not be so easy," Fargo said to draw his attention away from Antonia. "I've heard Reyes is a hard man to catch."

"Oh yes," Major Stalling said. "Reynaldo Reyes is as slippery as a greased rattlesnake. Knows the territory like the back of his hand. But I'll catch Reyes." Stalling spoke through gritted teeth. "I'll teach him not to rape white women, the filthy Mexican bastard. I'll teach him not to take money from white settlers. He'll pay. They'll all pay. Do you know where the hell we are?" he said to Fargo.

Stalling was beginning to sound like a madman.

"You tell me," Fargo said quietly. "Where are we?"

"This territory, Mr. Skye Fargo, is part of the United States of America," Stalling said, jabbing his finger in the air at Fargo. "And we won it. The U.S. Army won it in the war with those filthy Mexicans. Won it fair and square. Paid for every inch of it. In blood. And we won't have a bunch of dirty-skinned foreigners robbing settlers, raping our women, or telling us real Americans what to do."

Fargo whistled softly under his breath. So, Major Fox Stalling was a complete bigot. He had been Julio's second in command. Fargo could imagine how Major Stalling must have resented taking orders from Julio Delgado, who had been of mixed heritage—his ancestors had come from Spain, from Mexico, from an American settlement in Missouri, and an Indian pueblo in the Southwest.

But would Stalling's prejudice have been enough to drive him to murder his commander? And torture him? What about the rest of the men? They had followed Julio Delgado for many years. Delgado had been a powerful leader. It was hard to imagine what would make them put aside years of loyalty to turn against their colonel. Racism could be part of it. But what else?

"And just what do you think about all this Mexican slime in America, Mr. Trailblazer?" Stallings said. He looked at Fargo between slitted eyes as if measuring him.

Fargo shrugged. This wasn't the moment to pick a fight with Stalling.

"I understand you completely," he said noncommittally. Stalling seemed satisfied with his answer.

"Good man," Stalling said. "One of us real Americans." He looked over to where Antonia paced next to her roan, her face twisted with fury.

"Come along now, Señora Delgado," Fox Stalling called out. "We'll take you back to your hacienda. The badlands are dangerous. You'll need a U.S. Army troop to get home safely."

Stalling seemed awfully eager to have Antonia accompany them.

"No, *gracias*. I am heading the opposite direction, up to Dodge City," she lied.

Fargo wondered how far Stalling would push it. Had the troop really come north after the Reyes gang? Or was Stalling looking for Antonia Delgado? And Julio's box?

"But you cannot ride alone," Major Stalling protested. "What if Apaches or the Reyes gang found you on the trail?"

"I'll take that chance," Antonia said. "And Fargo will accompany me."

"Ha!" Stalling laughed. "One man, even the famous Trailsman, against Apaches and those *bandidos*. Ridiculous! I insist you come with us."

"No," Antonia said firmly, stamping her foot. "No."

"I think the lady has a right to make up her own mind," Fargo said quietly.

"Stay out of this, Fargo," Stalling said. "I command this troop and protect this territory. I say she comes with us."

"Commanding the troop doesn't mean ordering citizens around," Fargo pointed out.

"In time of threat to life and property, I have authority over any U.S. citizen in this territory," Stalling said. "In my judgment, the Reyes gang is a threat. Antonia Delgado, I order you to ride with us."

Fargo glanced about. One against three dozen men.

Lousy odds. But, when were the odds ever good? If he could just vault behind those rocks and get Antonia with him, they might back their way into the cleft and hold out there with Barney. But how long? How many of Stalling's troops could he take out before they got him? Lousy odds. But Fargo eased himself toward the rocks.

"I refuse to ride with you," Antonia said.

"Then I must insist," Stalling said, striding toward her.

"Jump, Antonia!" Fargo shouted, taking a shot at Stalling as he dove for the rocks. But the shot went wide and Stalling, rather than backing away from the gunshot, lunged toward Antonia. Fargo rolled once as he hit the ground and came up behind the rock, cursing as he saw that Stalling held Antonia round the waist. Damn. He hadn't expected Stalling would keep his head. The man was an experienced soldier. Fargo wouldn't underestimate him again. Antonia was between him and Stalling, but the tall man's head was unprotected. She was struggling, biting, and scratching. Fargo took careful aim at Stalling's face and tightened his finger on the trigger, waiting for a clear shot. Antonia screamed with rage, the sound echoing off the rocks.

Fargo saw a blur of movement pass him and a burly body hurled through space toward the struggling pair. Barney McCann had heard her scream, Fargo thought. McCann landed on the two, knocking them off their feet. Antonia broke free, rolled away, and ran to join Fargo behind the rock cover. He pulled her backward into the rock cleft.

Stalling and McCann rolled over, raining blows on one another. It was impossible to get a bead on Stalling. Several of the soldiers ran over and pulled McCann off their commander. Fox Stalling got to his feet. The soldiers held McCann by the arms as he straightened up. When they saw Barney McCann's face, the men holding him dropped his arms and fell back.

"What the hell?" Major Stalling shouted, fear in his voice. He stepped backward, his ruddy face as pale as if he had seen a ghost. He rubbed his eyes and looked again at McCann. "What the hell? I thought you were dead!"

Interesting, Fargo thought. He took careful aim at the major's left knee.

"No. Wait a minute. I want to hear what else he says to Barney. He knows something about my father's murder," Antonia whispered, pushing aside the barrel of the revolver.

They watched as Barney McCann stood looking down at the ground. Fargo saw the man begin to quake. His knees buckled and he slumped to the ground and lay still. Major Stalling and the soldiers stood in a half-circle around Barney as he lay still on the ground.

"He dead?" Stalling asked.

One of the men bent over.

"Nah."

"Get him on his feet," Stalling ordered sharply. Two men hauled up McCann. "Where have you been, McCann?" Stalling shouted into his face.

McCann whimpered.

"Answer me!" the major shouted, his face beet red.

A low gurgling sound came out of McCann.

Stalling poked McCann in the belly.

"He can't talk none, Major," one of the soldiers said.

Stalling laughed a short humorless bark and paced back and forth in front of McCann.

"Can't talk, eh? That it, McCann? Delgado's puppy

dog. Lost your master? Can't you say nothing? That your trouble?"

Fargo heard Antonia gasp as he tightened his finger on the trigger and took slow aim. But, Stalling suddenly grabbed McCann, drew his pistol and jammed it against the burly man's neck, turning so that McCann's big body shielded him from Fargo up in the rocks. He pushed McCann in front of him toward a nearby rock. The soldiers scattered, taking cover. Goddamn it, Fargo cursed to himself. He had missed his chance again.

"Okay, Fargo. Antonia," Stalling shouted. "The game's up."

"Let him go, Stalling," Fargo shouted back. "You can't shoot one of your own men."

"This man is a deserter," Stalling said. "I can have him hung anytime I damn well please. And I can have you arrested for hiding him. Come down right now. Or I blow his head off."

Antonia gasped again as they heard Stalling cock his pistol.

"I'll count three," Stalling said. "And then the rest of his brains get blown. One."

Fargo tried to find a clear shot. He could only see McCann's bandaged head and, from time to time, a little of Stalling's red hair behind. Stalling's hand holding his pistol? But no. The major was too careful. His hand was behind Barney's shoulder and he moved the burly man from side to side to keep Fargo from getting a good shot.

"What can we do? We've got to give up," Antonia said, the tears standing in her eyes. "But then he'll kill us all."

"Two."

"Goddamn it," Fargo cursed. There was nothing to do.

"I can't sit here and watch him kill Barney," Antonia said. She stood up and walked down toward Stalling. Fargo followed, throwing his pistol down on the ground. If he gave it up quickly, they might not search him and find the knife strapped to his ankle. There'd be another chance. There was always another chance. He watched carefully as the kid with bright blond hair picked it up and stored it in the right-hand saddlebag on a chestnut mare. Fargo would need it back later.

"I knew you'd see it my way," Stalling said. "Tie them up."

One of the men moved forward. Fargo held his wrists slightly apart as they were bound behind his back. The man tying him lashed the rope tight and turned away toward Barney McCann. Fargo relaxed his arms. Good. There was a little give in the ropes. It would be enough to work his hands free, but it would take him some time. He turned his back away from the rest of the men and began tugging and working at the ropes. The young blond man, the one Antonia had called Joe Strayhorn, was tying her arms.

"Joe. What's going on?" Fargo heard her whisper to the young man.

"Aw, Miz Delgado. It's been the awfullest things," the young man whispered back.

"What's going on over there?" Stalling snapped.

"Just tying up the prisoner. Sir," Strayhorn answered. He finished the job wordlessly and then backed away.

"Now that I have your full attention, señorita," Stalling said, pacing up and down in front of them, "I would like to ask you to return something to us. Something that, by rights, belongs to the troop. Something very valuable, which you have in your possession." Fargo thought about the map. He wondered where it was.

"I don't know what you're talking about, Major Stalling," Antonia spat back.

"Oh, but you do," Stalling answered. "I have reason to believe that you had a visit from a priest. A bald-headed priest."

"Have you seen Father Ernesto?" Antonia asked, fear edging her voice.

"Maybe so. Maybe not. All Catholics look alike to me," Stalling said. Several of the men chuckled. "Catholics are not real Americans. Are they, boys?"

"Nah, Major," one of the men said. Some of the others nodded.

"Catholics are foreigners. How do I know that? Because all the Catholics do is hoard money for that Italian pope. Ain't that so?" He stepped up close to Antonia.

She looked back at him steadily, her nostrils flaring with defiance.

"All those Catholics want is money. Money and gold. And silver. They want silver to send to that goddamn Italian king. It's all about silver, ain't it, señorita?"

"Lay off, Stalling," Fargo said.

"Gag him," Stalling said. "And check her saddlebags." One of the soldiers stepped forward and slipped Fargo's neckerchief over his mouth, tying it tightly behind his head. Another rummaged through Antonia's bags hitched to the roan.

"Found it!" the man said in a moment, coming forward with Julio's wooden box. "I found it, Major!"

Stalling greedily seized the box from the man's hands and tried to pry it open. The lock held.

He dropped the box onto the ground, drew his pistol and blasted the lock. Stalling leaned over and flipped open the top. He reached inside and pulled out a yellow silk sash with fringed edges, which unwound to its full length as he stood up.

"Well now, isn't that a pretty sight?" Stalling said. Fargo noticed that several of the men looked away. "Why this is a sash of valor. They gave this to some of the heroes of the war with Mexico. Now, what do you think old Julio Delgado was doing with one of these? Why, he would have been fighting his own kind in that war. How did your father feel killing his own kind?" he asked Antonia, throwing the yellow sash onto the ground behind him.

"My father was an American," Antonia said quietly. Fargo marveled at her control.

"Your father was a goddamned lying Mexican Catholic son of a bitch!" Stalling shouted at her.

She spit into his face and Stalling drew back his arm to hit her.

"Don't, sir," one of the men said. Fargo flicked his eyes over the troop, but he couldn't discern who had spoken. Stalling whirled about.

"Who said that?"

The men shifted. No one spoke.

"I said, who said that?" Stalling shouted, the flush creeping up his face like a wine glass slowly being filled.

"Come to attention, Private Carmichael!"

"Yes, sir!"

"Who spoke, Carmichael!"

"I don't know. Sir! I was busy listening to you. Sir!" Stalling turned back to Antonia.

"So, what else do we have here?" he said, bending over the box. He drew forth some papers and unfolded them, glancing at the pages one by one. When he had finished, he frowned, turned over the pages, rifled through them, and examined them again.

"So, where is it?" he said to Antonia, his bushy eyebrows lowered.

"I'll tell you again, Major Stalling. I don't know what you are talking about." She was a brave woman, Fargo thought. He remembered when the padre had surprised her in the shack the night before. She had hidden the map in her blouse. He wondered if it was still there.

"Well, let's see what this is," the major said. "Appears to be a letter. Maybe this will tell us." He peered at the pages.

"Who reads this Mexican shit?" he asked. Julio had obviously written to Antonia in Spanish, which Stalling couldn't read.

"I can, Major." One of the men stepped forward and removed some spectacles from his pocket, dusted them off, took the pages, and began to translate and read aloud.

"My dear daughter: I have asked our loyal friend, Padre Ernesto, to deliver this box to you. As I write these words, I hope that you will never have the chance to read them. If you are, it means that I am dead."

The man paused and looked up.

"Get on with it," Stalling said impatiently. Fargo saw the tears standing in Antonia's eyes as she heard her father's words being read aloud.

The man resumed.

"First, I must dispense with my worldly goods. The hacienda is yours, along with the cattle and horses. Please give each of the *vaqueros* a choice of the horses as a remembrance of me. Also, I have left a bag of gold in a safe at Fort Managa.

This is savings from my army pay which will be distributed to my men, who have fought loyally beside me for many hard and difficult years.

"Now, be brave, Antonia. For what I am about to tell you will be a burden. A burden which you did not ask for. I sent you away to New Orleans for your own protection. I will tell no one where you are, except for Padre Ernesto. And I pray to God that you will be safe there.

"But now that I am dead, danger is all around you. It began two weeks ago. You remember I visited the Mission Ascension to take them money . . ."

"What did I tell you?" Stalling cut in. "Always sending good American money over to that Italian pope."

"To take them money," the man continued reading, "to buy clothing for the orphans. Padre Ernesto was very grateful. He gave us a gift, a small pottery statue of Our Virgin Mary."

Fargo saw Stalling start and listen carefully to the words.

"The padre said this statue was very old and had been in the chapel as long as anyone could remember. The mission had a new, larger one. I brought the statue home, but as I was carrying it into the house, I had the bad luck to drop it. It broke into a thousand pieces. In the center, I found the map."

"Go on," Stalling said, excitement edging his voice. The man adjusted his spectacles.

"I have told no one about this map. Except for Barney. Now I am afraid I have put him in danger too. Yesterday we were speaking of it and I fear that another of the regiment overheard us, one that I do not trust and who does not follow me willingly. Many good men have died because of the curse of the Silver Maria. If it is God's will, I will be the next one. Remember this curse. Tell no one about this map, no matter how much you trust him.

"This map is the burden that I must now share with you. You will understand everything when you have examined it. This map rightly belongs to the Mission Ascension. You will know what to do."

"Uh, the rest is just other things," the man said, removing his spectacles. Fargo looked at the men about him. They looked ashamed. And guilty as hell.

"What did I tell you?" Stalling said in a loud voice. "The goddamn Mexicans always stick together. Delgado was going to find that treasure and give it to a bunch of squalling Mexican kids and Catholics. Or maybe he was really going to keep it all to himself. Do you think he was going to share that with us? Of course not."

"But he left you money," Antonia protested. "He left money for all of you. That was more than he had to do."

"Julio was just feeling guilty about cutting us out of the big one," Stalling said hotly. "And now, señorita, tell us where you've hidden the map."

"I wish I could tell you, Major Stalling," Antonia said levelly. She was good, Fargo thought. Real good. "But that's all there was in the box. Either Father

54

didn't put it in, or someone else took it out. That's all I know."

Stalling stepped back, watching her and rubbing his chin thoughtfully. She didn't blink or look away. After a long moment, Stalling sighed.

"Shit," the major said slowly with resignation. Stalling bought it, Fargo realized. He bought her story. "Almost got it," the major said as if to himself. "So close. Goddamn it." Stalling held his hand open before him and closed his fist on air. Fargo felt the hope rise in him. Maybe the major would figure the map was gone again. Lost. They might get out of this yet.

Stalling paced back and forth, his silver spurs clinking. The sound drew his attention and he looked down. The spurs were covered with dust. Absentmindedly, Stalling pulled a handkerchief from his pocket and bent down to polish them.

"Iver," a blurred voice said. Fargo felt the hope sink in him. Stalling looked up at Barney McCann.

"Iver," McCann said again, looking down at Stalling's now gleaming spurs.

"That's right, Barney," Stalling said, encouragingly. "Silver. So, you can talk."

4

Barney looked up at Major Stalling blankly.

"I bet you can talk just fine," Stalling said to Barney. He straightened up. "You can tell me where the silver is, can't you now? You know all about the treasure. Because your old friend Delgado told you all about it." He approached Barney, whose eyes widened with fear. His mouth opened again as if to speak, but no sound came out. Stalling raised his hand to strike McCann.

"Leave him alone!" Antonia cried out and Fargo cursed beneath the gag.

Stalling laughed.

"I think these three know something," he said, looking them over. "And I've got all the time in the world to find out."

"Major?" one of the men said tentatively.

"What?"

"Hadn't we better get a move on?" the man said. "The sun's getting low."

Stalling looked across the wide sage canyon, measuring the distances.

"Right," he said. "There's water back up this canyon. But, if we're going south, we have to get going. The next water is a good five hours' ride. Let's move."

Several of the men approached and untied Antonia's hands. She mounted her roan while one of the men held the bridle and they fetched a horse for Barney, too.

Nearby stood the young Joe Strayhorn. Fargo watched as the kid looked about furtively and then, when he thought no one was watching, bent down to pick up the yellow silk scarf from the ground. Strayhorn hastily wadded it up and shoved it inside his coat. Well, at least there was one man left who was still loyal to Julio Delgado. The man named Bill Carmichael approached.

"Where's your horse, Mr. Fargo?" he asked.

Fargo looked at him witheringly above his gag. The man loosened the neckerchief.

"It ran off," Fargo lied. During the last hour, he had seen the Ovaro from time to time, grazing nearby or standing half hidden in sagebrush, a short distance away. It would come when he whistled. But, Fargo thought, he'd leave the pinto free for the moment. He might need it later. When the regiment rode out, the pinto would follow, hanging back. If the soldiers saw it in the distance, they might think it was a wild pony. If they tried to catch it, the Ovaro would outrun any of their mounts. With luck, when it got dark he could slip away and call his horse.

"Too bad," said Carmichael. "You gotta have a horse in this territory. Up ahead of us, there's places where there's no drinking water you can walk to in a day. Or even two days. A man without a horse is a dead man."

"Ain't that the truth," Fargo said.

"We'll lend you one of our fast ones," said Carmichael with a grin. He led over a broken-down mare with swollen joints, her sharp bones almost poking through the dull gray coat. Carmichael started to untie Fargo's hands.

"Leave that one tied up," Stalling called out. "He's

a troublemaker." That's all right, Fargo thought to himself. He had worked the ropes loose enough that he could now almost slip his hands free.

Two of the men helped Fargo mount and the horse gave a shudder.

"I'm getting down," Fargo warned.

"What's the matter?" said Carmichael. "She's not good enough for you?"

"Problems under the saddle," Fargo said. He slid down from the horse unaided. Carmichael sighed impatiently and removed the worn saddle from the horse. Underneath, the saddle blanket had bunched up. He flung it aside.

"A galled horse is one sorry sight," Fargo muttered. "And unnecessary." The horse's back was spotted with oozing saddle sores.

"Shake out the blanket and smooth it down good," Fargo instructed. Carmichael did as he was told. Then he saddled the mare and straightened the girth.

"Cinch it tight and snug," Fargo said when he had been helped back onto the horse. At least the sores wouldn't be rubbed more. In a few days the horse's back would heal.

"Fall in!" Stalling called out. The U.S. Army didn't use a bugle call in the middle of Apache territory. The troop arranged itself. "Count fours! Prepare to mount!" There was a clanking of movement. "Mount! Fours right! March!"

Fargo found himself riding in the middle of the four columns, surrounded by soldiers. His old mare was tethered to the soldier in front of him. Antonia and Barney rode several horses ahead. It would be hard to escape. Almost impossible. Well, he thought, he might as well try to learn something about what had happened. He looked around.

Riding closest to him on his left was one of the men

that Antonia had greeted. Fargo had a vague memory of the man's face from the time, years before, when he had first met Julio Delgado.

"What's your name?" Fargo said pleasantly as they rode along.

The man glanced at him warily. His lined face was burned carmine from the glaring desert sun and a silver-flecked stubble roughened his cheeks. His blue Army-issue uniform was dust-dimmed and stained dark, here and there.

"Brent," he said. "Brent Fielding."

"Yeah," Fargo said. "I think I remember you from a long time ago." The memories came flooding back. "Weren't you the one on guard the time the Apaches crept up on us at dawn? Disguised as sagebrushes?"

Fielding's eyes crinkled as he smiled.

"Yep. That was me," he said. "Got myself a medal for that."

"Deserved it too," Fargo said. "We'd have all been killed if you hadn't been watching the bushes. How is the old Fort Managa?"

Brent Field's smile disappeared and his face hardened.

"Shit," Fielding said. "Used to be that Apache trouble was a sometime thing. Now, it's every day. Some stupid Army unit north of here double-crossed the local tribe. Kidnapped one of the Apache chiefs. Now all the tribes are on the warpath."

"Apaches are tough fighters, too," Fargo said.

"Damn good," said Fielding. "They swoop out of those mountain strongholds. They slaughter everybody at some lonely ranch. Then they disappear. We get there days later and we can't find 'em."

"And they're as tough as coyotes," Fargo said, remembering his many encounters with Apaches.

"And just as wily," Fielding added. "Good horse thieves. Hell, if we chase 'em and their horses give out, they just steal some more. If our horses break down, we gotta stop and parley with the settlers. And settlers don't want to sell their mounts. A lot of Apaches have gotten away from us that way."

"You got an Apache scout now," Fargo said, gesturing toward the Indian who rode impassively off to the side and toward the front of the troop.

"Yep. That was Major Stalling's idea. He's convinced that Indian's going to lead us to Apache hideouts."

"What do you think?" Fargo asked.

"I don't like it," Fielding answered. They rode in silence for a few minutes. "This is man-killing land," he said after a long time. "Sometimes we come across skeletons of battles that nobody will ever know about. Only these goddamn dry rocks have seen what happened. There's death all over the place. If it don't get you with a rattlesnake, it'll be a tomahawk. Or a bandit's bullet. Or a poison water hole."

Fargo nodded. Fort Managa was one of the loneliest and most godforsaken posts in the country. And one of the most dangerous.

"I remember what Julio used to say," mused Fargo. "He said this land made a man tough. Or it drove him crazy."

Fargo saw Brent Fielding stiffen.

"Look, mister," he said to Fargo, anger in his voice. "Let's get one thing straight. I'm a professional soldier. I do what I'm told." He looked away.

"Sorry," Fargo said. But Brent Fielding refused to say another word or look at him.

The trail had narrowed, winding between huge red boulders that littered the wide valley. The unit spread out, riding two by two. Fargo rode on the outside now, with Brent Fielding opposite him. He scanned the terrain, sighting a flash of white and black among the rocks. The Ovaro galloped alongside the troop, keeping far up on the distant hillside. The sky was pale blue, as if faded by the glaring sun. Three vultures flew overhead and dove down, just off the trail up ahead on Fargo's side.

Must be a fresh kill, Fargo thought. Only a few hours old. Then, as the realization exploded in his mind, he gritted his teeth and swore under his breath. Goddamn it. Goddamn.

Between the boulders he glimpsed a shallow dry arroyo, obscured by mesquite. He could see the black wings of the big birds flapping from time to time. He would have to find out. He had to know.

In another moment he would be opposite where the vultures had descended. This would be his only chance. If he broke away to look, they would think he was escaping. And they might shoot.

He was four horse lengths from a break between the rocks that would take him down into the arroyo. With a final tug, he slipped the ropes from around his wrists and waited, muscles tense. Three lengths. Two. One.

He reached forward and slipped the bridle from the mare's head, slapped her on the neck, and turned her head with his hands. She hesitated. He slapped her again and she turned, stumbling down the trail between the rocks, gravity giving her speed. He heard a shout behind him as some of the men turned off the trail in pursuit. The mare headed between stands of mesquite and then burst out onto the flat open bottom of the arroyo. The startled vultures flew into the air and then perched not far away, watching.

Padre Ernesto lay next to his dead mule, the bloodstain of a bullet wound darkening the front of his robe and the sand beneath him. His eyes were open and his face expressionless. One of his hands grasped his rosary. The flies buzzed around. The contents of his saddlebags were strewn on the ground. Fargo turned away just as the soldiers rode up, guns drawn. They looked nervously at one another when they saw what Fargo had seen.

"Should we shoot him?" one said, aiming at Fargo.

"Leave him alone," said Brent Fielding. "Tie him up tight this time. Get him back in line."

As they were riding back up toward the column, Fargo heard Fielding muttering to himself. "Goddamn death all over the place," Fielding said.

Fargo knew he would not tell Antonia what he had seen. Not now. Not for a long time.

The hot red ball of sun sank into the hazy horizon. They came to a halt for the night on the banks of Bitter Creek. Fargo's mare followed as the soldiers reined into a circle and dismounted. Fargo slid down off his horse and spotted Antonia. She walked over. The soldiers ignored them. Some bustled about unsaddling the horses, leading them to water and to graze. Others gathered wood and lit campfires.

"I saw you try to get away," she whispered.

"I wanted to see something just off the trail," Fargo said.

"Oh," she said. He heard the relief in her voice. She had been worried he would abandon her. "What did you find?"

"Tell you later," he whispered back. "I'm getting us out of here. Tonight. Watch for me. Don't sleep."

She nodded.

"Move on," he said, aware that some of the men had noticed them talking. Fargo walked off and sat down beside a rock, watching the soldiers pitch camp.

"Can I go down to the creek to wash up?" she

asked one of the men standing nearby. Stalling appeared and heard her question.

"Wash up all you want," the major said. "In fact, take a nice long bath. That's something all of us would like to see." Several of the men laughed. She turned away and walked down toward the water. Stalling watched her go, stroking his chin.

"Carmichael!" he called.

"Sir!"

"Pitch the tent for our guest."

"Yes. Sir!"

Stalling moved away and several of the soldiers brought out the rolled canvas.

"He hardly ever uses the tent," complained one of the men.

"Yeah, but we hardly never have ladies in camp," the other said.

"Where are we going to pitch this danged thing?" a tall skinny one asked.

Fargo looked about.

"How about on that sandy spot there?" Fargo suggested, nodding his head. "It's real level."

"Why, thank you," the skinny one said, as they began to lay out the canvas and pound in the stakes.

Fargo neglected to tell the soldiers that the spot was also right next to a clump of sage. If he needed to creep up on the tent in the middle of the night, it would be easier under cover of a bush.

Another soldier, tired and dragging his boots, led several horses by on the way to the creek. One of them was a chestnut mare. The one with his Colt revolver in the saddlebag.

"Hey, you," Fargo called out. The man looked up at him, bleary-eyed. "Don't mean to meddle. But don't you unsaddle those horses before they're watered?"

The man looked back at the horses and shrugged.

"Sure. I guess," he said. He slowly untied the diamond hitches binding the packs to the *apperajos*. Then he unsaddled them and dropped all the gear in a pile on the ground. Without looking back at Fargo, he walked on.

The saddlebag with his Colt inside was ten feet in front of him. Fargo smiled to himself. He rubbed his ankles together, feeling the knife strapped around his ankle. He'd only have to wait. And watch.

The blue dusk gathered and the golden campfires flickered. Fargo dozed. And watched. After a while, Bill Carmichael approached and yanked him to his feet and began to untie his hands.

"You get some grub. And some water," Carmichael said. "Then we truss you up for the night."

"Sounds fine by me," Fargo said, letting himself be led to the campfire. He spotted Antonia and the major sitting at another fire. The major was laughing. Antonia was not.

Fargo sat down in the circle of soldiers. The Army-issue hardtack was almost inedible. He took a bite, then slid it inside his shirt. He managed to hide away four more pieces. But the beans were tasty. So was the coffee. Fargo drank lots of it. It would be a long night.

Afterward, Carmichael led him back to a spot near the tent. Barney McCann lay nearby, tied up. Carmichael pinioned Skye's arms. Once again, Fargo held his wrists apart, resisting the rope, but Carmichael knew that trick.

"Bring 'em together, Fargo," he said, drawing the rope tighter. Fargo stopped resisting. Carmichael bound his ankles too, as he lay down on the ground. Then he covered Fargo with a blanket and threw his hat over his head.

"Sweet dreams," Carmichael said with a chuckle

as he moved back toward the campfire. Fargo began immediately. He moved his head from side to side until the hat shifted slightly and he could see out from under the brim. The men were all around the fires. No one was watching

He rolled onto his side and coiled his long, lean body backward, bending his knees, reaching down with his hands to pull up the leg of his jeans. He had to struggle, the tight ropes making the movement almost impossible.

He felt about for the handle of the knife. There. Slowly, slowly, he slipped the throwing knife out of the ankle sheath. If he were to drop it, it would fall by his legs and be almost impossible to reach.

Just then he heard voices approaching.

"Who's on guard duty tonight?" one of the voices said.

"Strayhorn. And Brent Fielding too," said a high-pitched voice. That was good news, he thought. Strayhorn was loyal to Delgado. Fielding was a loyal soldier, but a rational man. If they caught him escaping, he might be able to talk his way out of it.

"Hey, you!" he heard Stalling call out. "Check that prisoner!"

"Does he mean us?" one of the men said under his breath. "C'mon."

Fargo reluctantly let go of the knife and felt it fall beside his leg. He straightened out, covering the blade with his knee, and lay still.

The men paused beside him.

"Looks okay to me," the high-pitched voice said.

"Uncover him," the other said. "Check his ropes." Fargo felt the blanket pulled back.

"Easy, boys," Fargo said, as they turned him on his side. He was careful to move his leg to hide the knife. One of them tugged at the ropes.

"That Carmichael does nice knots. Real tight," Fargo said. "Ought to be a sailor." One of the men chuckled and they covered him up and left him alone.

As soon as they were out of hearing, Fargo coiled himself up again and began to strain against the ropes, fumbling for the knife which lay just out of reach of his fingertips on the ground. Damn Carmichael, he thought. He did tie good knots.

Fargo heard a roar of laughter and then Major Stalling's voice above the others, coming closer.

"Yes, I had the tent put up for you, señorita." Fargo looked out from under the brim of his hat and saw Stalling and Antonia walking toward the tent.

"How long will it take to get me home?" Antonia asked him, coldness in her voice.

"As long as it takes to find out what I want," said Stalling.

"I tell you. I know nothing about this map!"

"I think you do," he said, stepping close to her. He grabbed her suddenly, pulling her toward him, one hand on her breast, trying to kiss her. She struggled, elbowing and scratching his face.

"Bitch!" he yelled, and stepped back, holding his cheek. "You've got nails like a hellcat."

"Leave me alone," she said, no fear in her voice. She had a lot of grit in her, Fargo thought.

"Sure," Stalling said. "For tonight. But tomorrow, you're going to tell me about the map. Or one of your friends will. And, eventually, you'll give me what I want." Fargo heard her light footsteps and he shifted slightly and saw her enter the tent. After a few seconds a lantern lit the interior and Stalling moved back toward the campfire.

Fargo strained again and brushed the handle of the knife with his fingertips, then he stretched, grasping it between two fingers and easing it into his hand. Not pausing for an instant, he turned the blade toward his wrists and, manipulating it gently with the tips of his fingers, began to saw through the ropes. The sharp blade sliced through the strands and he felt the bonds loosen. His hands were free. He quickly cut through the ropes binding his ankles. He gathered the lengths of rope, wound them into a coil and looped his belt through it. He felt about with his right hand and found a large, smooth rock that fit well in the palm of his hand. Then he straightened out and lay still.

Bill Carmichael arrived to stand guard outside the tent. He sauntered over to where Fargo lay. Fargo felt about with his other hand and found a small pebble.

"Comfy?" Carmichael said.

"Softest bed in the territory," Fargo answered from under his hat. He eased his hand out from under the blanket on the far side and flicked the pebble toward some bushes. The pebble clinked on a rock.

"What was that?" Carmichael said, walking a few steps toward the sound. Fargo was on his feet in a second and the rock in his right hand caught Bill Carmichael on the back of the skull. The man slumped to the ground and Fargo sank down with him, cradling Carmichael's fall. He quickly laid the unconscious man flat out, covered him with the blanket, and positioned his hat over his face. In another moment his Colt was in his hand and he was melting into the shadow of the sagebrush beside the tent.

Fargo drew his knife and made a careful and small slit in the fabric. He had to slice the canvas very slowly or it would make a tearing sound. He peered in and saw Antonia undressing, her back to him. He lengthened the slit.

"Antonia," he whispered. She turned, her blouse clutched to her, but not hiding her full, round breasts with their dark delicate nipples. Her worried face brightened as she recognized him. Wordlessly, she donned her clothes. While she was dressing, he slipped inside the tent and tied shut the front tent flaps, top to bottom, double-knotting them on the inside. Then he arranged the blankets so it appeared that she was in the bedroll. That would slow them down a few moments if they came inside to check on her. Moments could make a difference. He put out the lamp and they slipped through the slit in the back of the tent.

It was an easy matter to sneak away to the edge of the camp, following the line of sage. They were almost to the periphery, when Antonia stopped.

"I can't go without Barney," she said.

Fargo considered their chances. Every second they delayed increased the likelihood they'd be caught. And Barney McCann was a big man, awkward, unpredictable.

"He was loyal to my father," said Antonia.

"Stay here," Skye said. "I'll give it a try." He slipped back toward the tent. Two men stood outside the tent looking toward the campfires. Carmichael lay still in Fargo's bedroll. He wouldn't remain unconscious for long. Keeping his eye on them, Fargo crawled over to where Barney lay. He cut the ropes binding his hands and leaned over the inert man.

"Barney. Keep quiet. If you want to help Antonia, follow me." The man did not appear to have heard him. Fargo started to shake his shoulder, but Barney rolled over and sat up. He stood slowly and followed Fargo without a sound. On their way back to Antonia, Fargo saw two canteens beside some bedrolls. He grabbed them. They were both full. God bless the professional soldier, he thought. The golden rule of the army was: Fill your canteen first.

He remembered that Joe Strayhorn and Brent

Fielding were on guard duty. They might be persuaded to look the other way while Fargo culled a couple of horses for Barney and Antonia. He motioned Antonia and Barney to stay in the shadows, and sighting Strayhorn by the corral, he moved forward.

Just then he heard voices.

"Hey, Joe!" Two soldiers strode into sight. Fargo melted back into the darkness.

"Over here."

"All quiet?" one asked.

"Not a sound," Strayhorn said. "How's things . . . up in camp."

"Ole Major's getting drunk. Talking about what he's going to do to Delgado's daughter in the morning," the first one said.

"Shit," Strayhorn said.

"Oh, don't take it so hard," the second one said. "She's just a woman. And a Mexican to boot."

"She's Colonel Delgado's daughter!" Strayhorn said hotly. "Since when have you forgotten him?"

"Since Stalling came along and pointed out what a goody-goody Delgado was," the first answered. "Stalling's right, you know. Delgado was faking it. He really only cared about his own people. The Mexicans. He wasn't a real American. That map thing proved it."

"Yeah, but Jesus. Stalling went and murdered him!"

"We didn't see it. So, we don't know that for sure. Aw, lighten up, Strayhorn. You're off guard duty now anyway. We're taking over." Strayhorn walked away and Fargo rejoined Antonia and Barney. He could tell from her face in the dim light that she had heard the men's conversation. It explained a lot.

With two of the men guarding the horses, it would be harder to spirit away two mounts. And every second counted. Just then he heard shouting from the direction of the tent. Their escape had been discovered.

"There's trouble up in camp," one of the guards shouted to the other.

"Watch the horses! Look sharp, now."

There was no time to lose. They would have to go on foot. Fargo motioned to Barney and Antonia and they slipped around the stand of sage and out onto the open plain. He hurried them along into the night, hearing the shouting of the soldiers behind them. On they ran, and he heard Antonia becoming winded. Barney was slow but seemed to be holding up. They were almost out of earshot of the camp. Fargo looked about. They had run up a gentle slope, bumpy with sage and mesquite. All was quiet around them, the uproar of the camp a distant buzz. He whistled, listened, and heard nothing.

"Come on," he said. They pushed themselves further up the slope. When Antonia's panting was loud and ragged, Fargo stopped again. He whistled. This time he heard a low nicker, far off, and in another moment, the sound of hooves. The Ovaro galloped toward them and came to a halt, nuzzling Fargo.

"Hey, fella," Fargo said, stroking his nose. "So you missed me?" The pinto whinnied low. "Get on. Quickly." He said to Antonia and Barney. They set off, continuing to climb the long slope up to the top of the ridge, Fargo running beside his horse.

It was hard going. Skye felt the breath ripping his throat and the heaviness of his legs as he fought to keep them pumping. They had to make some distance. A few miles. Just a few miles.

Then something happened. His legs felt lighter somehow, weightless. He found himself thinking about the part of him that was Indian blood and about the way the Indians loped gracefully over the plains, for miles and miles and miles.

His mind was a dark quietness as he ran on. The few thoughts came slowly to him, outlined with a clear light.

In this country a man without a horse is a dead man.

Wild ponies ran in the canyons ahead.

Tomorrow he would find some.

And the Diablo cutoff lay ahead.

Man-killing land.

No one would believe they would attempt it on foot. And he heard another thought in Brent Fielding's voice.

Goddamn death is all over the place.

5

The Trailsman's lake blue eyes swept the land before him as he stood on the top of the bluff, washed by the pale light of dawn. Below him it was still night, the blue shadows filling the bowl of the sage. He spotted a curving ruffle of tall grasses in the lowest depression of the valley before him. If water was around, it would be down there.

He turned and looked back over the low dry hills. Still no sign of pursuit. On the Ovaro, Antonia and Barney hunched over, half-asleep.

Fargo started forward down the rocky slope, walking briskly now, the pinto following. His throat was raw from the night's run but his long, lean body felt light and warmed. They had made twenty miles. Twenty miles of zigzagging through dark canyons and across nameless flats. Running, then walking, then running again beside his horse. He needed a rest now, he thought. So did the pinto. A few hours by the water, in the tall grasses, and they would be ready to go on.

A tight, compressed smile played across his lips as he thought of the regiment. The three of them would be hard to track. He had made sure of that. During the long night, he had led them over every rock field and gravel pit along the way. It would take a good tracker a lot of effort to pick up their trail.

But there was the Apache scout.

Apaches were notorious as trackers, Fargo thought. Some said they did it by smell. Whatever it was, Apaches had an uncanny sense of any living creature moving across this vast desert land. The only hope was to keep moving. And maybe, just maybe, after a day or two, Stalling would give up the chase.

He walked now across the sage plain of the valley floor, the grasses just ahead. Fargo saw the promising darkness of the green leaves. A few low bushes. Water. No question.

He worked his way in among the grasses and leaves, followed by the Ovaro. They broke out into a small clearing beside a small trickle of water running over the brown stones. He threw himself down beside the stream and drank long. The pinto lowered its muzzle into the water beside him. The water tasted of minerals, but it was cool, wet. He dashed it over his head and neck, feeling now his exhaustion. As he rolled away from the stream onto his back and he closed his eyes, he saw Antonia dismounting.

It was hot when Fargo awoke. He rubbed his face and sat up, looking about him. Barney McCann lay nearby, sleeping heavily, and Antonia was curled up on her side. The Ovaro nibbled at the grasses. Fargo rose and stretched the stiffness out of himself and Antonia stirred.

She sat up, looking about her as if trying to remember where she was. When she saw him she jumped to her feet and came over to put her arms around him.

"How can I ever thank you for getting us away from that horrible man?" she said. Fargo held her close and she seemed to melt into him.

"We're not away yet," he cautioned her, stroking her hair. "They could be tracking us. And there's a chance they could find us."

"What are we going to do?" He looked down and wished they were alone. Alone and in some safe place.

"Well, with the pinto between the three of us, we sure can't outrun them," he said. "Of course, they don't know we have a horse. They think we're on foot. That's to our advantage."

"Why?"

"They'll confine their search to the immediate area around the camp. At least for the first few hours. It will take them a while to pick up our trail. Following us won't be easy. I hope." He didn't mention his fears about the Apache scout.

"But, Skye," she said, looking up at him and running her fingers along his jawline. "How long can you keep on running like this?"

"As long as it takes," he said. "But if we're lucky, it won't be too much longer. There are wild horses in these canyons up ahead. Maybe we can rope in a couple. How's your riding?"

"Father taught me to break horses when I was a girl," Antonia answered.

"Good," Fargo said. "Because you and I will have to ride the wild ones. Barney's not up to it." He rummaged in the saddlebag and pulled out his extra jeans.

"See if you can fit into these," he said, tossing them to her. "That skirt will be in the way for rough riding."

"*Gracias*," she said, catching them midair. She disappeared into the bushes and changed as they continued talking.

"And then? Where will we go?" she said, as the leaves rustled.

"You tell me," Fargo said.

There was a silence. She was debating with herself whether to tell him about the map, he thought.

"Skye . . . I . . . I am afraid that if I tell you, it will only bring you trouble." she began.

"It's already brought me trouble," he said.

"That is true," she admitted. "But will you just trust me for a while? Until I feel I can tell you?" She stepped out of the bushes in his jeans. Her hair was tucked up under her hat, her blouse tucked in. She could almost pass for a Mexican boy, Fargo thought, except for her curves.

"Put this on, too," he said, throwing her a vest.

"Por que?"

"Makes you look more like a boy," Fargo said shortly, thinking about Reynaldo Reyes and his gang. She raised her eyebrows but didn't ask questions.

"Good," Fargo said, surveying the results. "Now, I said I'd try to help you. I promised Padre Ernesto." He thought of the priest lying beside the trail. Goddamn Stalling. "So, since you're not going to tell me what this burden is, you'd better tell me where we're going."

"To the heart of the country," she said, as if afraid of the sound of the words.

"Even though the regiment will be heading that way, back to Fort Managa?"

"I must," she said.

"I figured," he said slowly. He thought about her words to Padre Ernesto. She planned to save the Mission Ascension from the wealthy landowner. And it had to do with the map. He could guess what the connection was. But he'd bide his time, wait for her to tell him. "The regiment could be on our tail any minute," he said. "If we can find horses, our best chance is to take the Diablo cutoff."

Her eyes flashed questions and fear.

"The Diablo? But that is the most dangerous trail in the world! No one makes it through the Diablo, except bandits and Apaches. There's no water. The trail is not marked. It would be . . . it would be suicide to go there."

"It would be suicide not to," he said. "If the regiment picks up our tracks leading south, they'll figure we're planning to follow the Pecos River trail. They'll never expect us to attempt the Diablo."

"I guess you're right," she said. "How will you know which way to go?"

"I've been through the Diablo," he said. "A long time ago. I think I can remember the trail. It's rough. But we'll make it."

"I trust you completely," she said. "Still . . . the Diablo." She shivered, despite the hot sun.

"Let's get a move on," he said, turning toward the horse. He was pleased to see that Antonia had remembered to unsaddle the pinto before she rested.

While Antonia woke Barney and led him toward the stream for another drink, Fargo went through his saddlebags. There was the hardtack he had stolen from camp. A little coffee, flour, and lard. Some pemmican. Not much for the three of them to go on.

He gave Antonia and Barney each a piece of the hardtack and the pemmican and took some for himself. He made sure the pinto took another draught and then emptied the canteens into the stream.

"What are you doing?" Antonia asked. She watched him begin to refill them from the stream.

"After a day or two in the canteens, water is almost undrinkable," he answered. "Tastes like hell. Every chance you get, you freshen it up."

She nodded, rose, and helped Barney back onto the pinto. Fargo led them out of the deep brush, pausing at the edge to scan the wide hilltops that lay all around.

Suddenly he didn't like this valley. They were too

exposed. Anyone coming over a hill from miles around would sight them here. He hurried them across the sage toward the cover of the low foothills. But, all the while, he continued to glance behind him. Nothing. Yet.

The land changed suddenly in the space of a few miles. One moment they were rounding a boulder-strewn hillside, woolly with gray sage. The next moment they were crossing a red dust flat, carved with the braiding of dried-up rivulets. Fargo saw the tall rock spires of the badlands in the distance, where the head of the Diablo cutoff lay.The hot wind kicked up the dust into his face.

Fargo pulled his neckerchief up over his mouth and nose as he walked into the dry wind. He motioned for Antonia to do the same for her and Barney. It blew harder, swirling about them, and Fargo leaned into it, his pace slowed. They seemed to be inching across the wide flat, he thought. Then he let his mind go dark again, concentrating on his legs as he broke into a slow trot against the wall of wind. A whistling noise rose about them. The pinto whinnied nervously.

The sun was a soft, white coin hanging in the dirty brown sky. Fargo peered ahead, into the haze. All about them the dust spun crazily. The whistling noise grew louder, became a roar.

"Hold on!" he yelled suddenly. He grabbed the bridle of the pinto and fought crosswise against the wind, heading for the cover of some nearby red rocks.

The whirlwind hit them with a stunning force, and he felt his feet being swept out from under him. He heard Antonia scream and Barney cry out, the sounds muffled by their scarves, the dust and the howling wind. Fargo hit the ground and struggled to his feet. He pushed his way along the side of the horse and pulled Antonia and Barney off its back. The pinto reared and broke away. Fargo pulled them toward the rock cover, struggling with Barney, who wanted to follow the pinto. Finally, he wrestled him over to the rock, where they hunched down. The gusts blasted the stinging sand onto their cheeks for long moments more and then the sound diminished.

"*Dio!*" Antonia exclaimed.

"Dust devil," Fargo said. "Big one. Luckily they don't last long."

"Why is everything in this land called the devil?" Antonia said. "Dust devils, the Diablo cutoff. There are devils everywhere."

The wind had calmed and blew steadily now. The sky brightened again above them. Fargo stood and pulled Antonia to her feet. Barney stood also. Antonia looked down. Dust caked her trousers and her vest. She brushed them off and looked up. Her brows, lashes, and hair were whitened with the grit, her face powdered with it.

"If you could see yourself," Fargo said, chuckling.

"Same to you," she said, laughing with him. Barney caught the sound and laughed as well, a low, humorless pulse of sound. Fargo whistled and the pinto came running. They shook the dust from them as best they could and moved on through the long, hot afternoon.

A few miles before the Diablo cutoff, Fargo's keen hearing picked up the sound of a distant whinny. He saw the pinto's nostrils flare.

"Get down," he ordered Antonia and Barney. No time to explain. He pulled them quickly off the Ovaro and swung up into the saddle, galloping off toward the mouth of a red rock canyon. As he rode, he wound his ropes and readied them, along with two bridles.

Sure enough, he thought. As he neared he could

see the small herd of wild Appaloosas grazing on the floor of the canyon in the late afternoon shadow. The herd was upwind, so that he could get very close without the horses smelling the human scent. Fargo flattened himself against the neck of the pinto, which slowed and trotted toward the herd. He would have to get in among them before trying to rope them. Bringing in two wild ponies at once was going to be a real trick.

They were beautiful beasts, their spotted coats unbranded and wide hooves unshod. They tossed their manes in the wind as they moved restlessly over the plain, their necks bent down in search of tender grasses among the sun-seared mesquite.

As they drew close, Fargo picked out two nearby which looked strong. He tensed his muscles and the Ovaro, feeling his readiness, paused. He raised up in a fluid motion and sent the first rope lasso spinning into space, a wavering circle of rope arcing out against the sky and suddenly falling around the neck of a spotted mare. He drew the rope tight with one hand, while sending the second lasso aloft with the other. The mare, feeling the rope around her neck, reared, and the second Appaloosa, mottled with reddish brown, shied away. The second lasso fell against its flank and the herd suddenly panicked, turning to gallop up the canyon.

"Son of a bitch!" Fargo swore, as the mare tugged at the rope, rearing again and again. As the herd ran away, he tried to get the mare to follow the pinto, pulling on the line. But she balked. They had to have two horses to survive the trail, he thought. Only one thing to do.

Fargo jumped down from the pinto and, holding the rope firmly, approached the wild Appaloosa. He made a low clucking noise and she quieted a little. He came nearer. Then he suddenly dashed forward and threw the bridle over her head, jerking it harshly. As she took off, Fargo made a flying leap and scrambled up onto her back.

As soon as she felt the weight of him, she reared and bucked. Fargo held on to the rope as the scenery whirled around him and he dug his knees into her flank. He jerked again on the bridle, bringing her head down hard and she calmed a little. She was still galloping, shifting directions every few strides, but he was glad to see they were heading up the canyon after the rest of the herd.

After a few minutes Fargo felt the horse relax under him. He patted her neck and loosened his grip on the bridle slightly. She responded with more speed. She wasn't completely wild. The mare had been ridden before, he was sure of it. Probably an Apache horse which had broken loose. Luck was with him. He looked about and saw the Ovaro running alongside them at some distance. Fine. Everything was going fine.

The herd was running ahead of them, but the pace was slowing as they felt the danger far behind. Fargo tightened his knees on the mare and she edged up close to the group, running just a few strides behind a muscular stallion. Fargo let fly the lasso again and it snagged the horse. Fargo slowed the mare gradually, the stallion resisting the rope's pull as the rest of the herd pulled away. Finally, he brought the mare around, turning her nose slowly until the two horses galloped back down the canyon.

He found Antonia and Barney in the shade on one side of a large bolder. Fargo dismounted, holding the ropes tightly. He had been gone almost two hours. The sun was about to set. They were losing time. The head of the Diablo cutoff was just ahead.

"We can't stay here," he said. "Let's get a move on."

While Antonia held the Appaloosas, Fargo helped Barney onto the pinto. "Take the mare," he said to Antonia.

He bridled the stallion and mounted. The horse shot away while he clutched the bridle and wound his hands into the thick mane. He looked back. The pinto followed. And Antonia brought up the rear. She was riding well, he saw. She did a lot of things well. And she kept her head. She would need to if they were going to get through the Diablo cutoff alive.

Fargo dug the toe of his boot into the crack and lifted the jagged piece of dried mud. Even in the late twilight he could see that underneath was dust. Dry as a bone.

"Last chance?" Antonia said, eyeing the broken-down wagon bed on which someone had scrawled "Last Chance Water."

"No chance," Fargo said, gazing across the cracked dry earth. He narrowed his eyes and scanned the jagged rock gate through which they would pass into the Diablo cutoff.

"We go that way," he said, pointing. Antonia shivered and drew close to him.

"It looks like the gates of hell," she said.

"It is," he said. "But there's no other way."

"What about the water?" she asked.

"Two canteens," he said. "Minus a little. We ration. One swallow three times a day. If we make good time we'll have enough." Barely, he thought, but he kept that to himself.

"Then, let's go," Antonia said. They swung into their saddles again. Barney, who had not dismounted, rode between them. Fargo thought again how lucky he was to have the pinto. Even with the bulky man on its back, it did not hesitate, seeming to know just where to go. The Appaloosas gave them more trouble. Instinct told the horses that there was no water up ahead. They balked and started as Fargo and Antonia guided them up the rocky trail and between the towering red rocks onto the trail of the Diablo cutoff.

They rode for another mile. The rising moon, waxing toward one quarter, threw light on the weird and fantastic rock shapes looming above them.

He was looking for the cliff, a safe camping place, and a good lookout point he dimly recollected from long ago. There were lots of cliffs and caves in this country. Most of them full of Apaches or cougars. Finally, it came into view up ahead. Fargo scouted to assure that it was empty and safe, then led them up a long rise to the protected rock overhang. Antonia and Fargo dismounted at once. Barney got down heavily. Fargo picketed the horses securely, patting their flanks and hunting about for some grasses. He found only a few handfuls which the horses nosed gratefully.

No water for three days, he thought as he fed them. Unless they were lucky and found a water hole. But he wouldn't count on that. Without water and ridden hard, the horses would be half dead by the time they got through. He curried the Ovaro, very slowly, for the hell of it, wondering if he had made the right decision.

Antonia had laid out the bedrolls and Barney had fallen onto one. He was already snoring. They moved a short distance away so that they would not wake him.

"He fell asleep before I even gave him water," Antonia said, gesturing toward the canteens.

"He'll wake up thirsty," Fargo said. He rifled in the

saddlebags for their supper. They wouldn't risk a fire. He tossed her some pemmican, which she caught and bit into without hesitation.

He grinned. Some women would have protested at that, he thought. Not Antonia. If he had to be on the Diablo with a woman, he was damned lucky it was Antonia Delgado, daughter of Julio. The thin desert air was getting cold. Antonia shivered and wrapped the bedroll about her. Fargo sat down beside her and put his arm about her shoulders. She nestled close to him.

"You haven't asked me what this is all about," she said quietly.

"I did ask. Back at Loyal Gulch," Fargo said. "And you said you'd tell me when you could."

"It's about the map," she said, hesitantly. That much he knew, he thought, but he kept silent. Waiting. "Have you ever heard of the Silver Maria?" she asked. A vague memory stirred in his mind.

"The Silver Maria," he said, as if tasting the words. "Isn't that some legend down south?"

"Yes, in the heart of the country," Antonia said. "But it is more than a legend. You see, three hundred years ago, a band of conquistadors came through this land. The conquistadors were the armed guard for some monks who came to found a mission for the Indians. The monks brought a special icon from Rome. It was to be the centerpiece of this mission, this great cathedral in the desert."

"The Silver Maria?"

"*Sí.* An exquisite replica of our Virgin Mother, made of pure silver and covered with jewels. The Silver Maria was supposed to protect the monks in the new land."

"Some protection," Fargo said.

"Exactly. Very soon, the conquistadors became

greedy. They wanted to melt down the Silver Maria and divide her between themselves. The monks got wind of the plot, and with the help of some Indians, they hid the Silver Maria and drew a map. Then the map was lost."

"And Julio found it inside the pottery statue at the mission," Fargo said.

"Sí."

"And Julio, being Julio Delgado, planned to find the Silver Maria and save the mission and the orphanage," Fargo said. Antonia nodded.

"Sí. You see, my mother died when I was born," she said, crossing herself. "And my father could not take care of me alone. So, I grew up at Mission Ascension. It is my home."

"And you would save the mission too," Fargo said to her, adding, ". . . *if* you had the map."

She smiled at him and raised her hand to the front of her blouse, undoing the buttons slowly. He watched as the blouse opened and he saw her deep cleavage and swelling curves. She reached inside and drew out the map, as he knew she would. Almost before he realized what he was doing, his hand reached forward.

She recoiled, watching him warily. He smiled.

"I'm just curious," he said. She shook her head.

"There is a curse on the Silver Maria," she said. "This is what my father meant when he wrote to trust no one. You see, the desire to possess the Silver Maria corrupts men. It turned the conquistadors against the monks."

"And your father's troops against him," Fargo added. "Are you afraid that I will turn against you?" She regarded him in the moonlight and then he saw her relax.

"No. No, I do not think so. Let us look at this together."

Fargo rose and searched in his saddlebags, finding the candle that the priest had given him to search the shack for scorpions. He lit it with his tinderbox and sat down beside her, holding the candle above the map spread out on the ground.

The writing was faded, but he could easily see the lines indicating a river which looked like the Pecos and twisted lines like mountains. A deep red cross was drawn along one of the snaking lines, which seemed to indicate a canyon.

"What's this say?" he asked, pointing to the faded inscription.

"It is written in old Spanish," Antonia said, "and hard to translate. But this is what I think it means." She began to read as she traced the words with one finger. "In the grave, like a snake, go forward and take the left-hand canyon. Past the chimney and the needle's eye. Go for one hour and you have gone almost nowhere. Under the lonely green arms, the Silver Maria waits for the man with a pure heart." Antonia fell silent and the words seemed to echo in the night. The moon hung in the black velvet sky. It reminded him of the time passing. By the next new moon, the landowner would repossess the mission unless he and Antonia could find the Silver Maria.

"Count me in," he said. "For the Mission Ascension."

She exhaled a sigh and he realized she had been holding her breath. He tightened his arm around her and she looked up at him, her black eyes shining in the candlelight. She turned her face away and blew out the flame, then turned back.

Skye bent his head down to kiss her, long and deeply, savoring again her sweet flavor. Antonia hummed, deep in her throat, a kind of purr as he ran his hands up her back. She reached up and loosed the clip from her hair so that it cascaded all about her shoulders. He ran his hands through her long heavy tresses as he explored her mouth, feeling her suck on his tongue. He twisted her hair in his hands, silken, cool as the night, rubbed it against her neck. She purred again and drew away for a moment to unbutton the rest of her blouse.

"Oh, *mi amor*, I have waited so many years for tonight," she breathed. "You were the hero of all my girlhood fantasies." Her blouse fell open and he saw her large round breasts with sharp, delicate, dark nipples, crinkled with desire. She pulled the blouse down around her shoulders and off. Then, with a sudden movement, she lunged forward, pushing him backward underneath her.

"I'm not going to resist," he murmured into her shoulder. She arched her back so that her large breasts hung over his face, and she rotated her shoulders so that they brushed his eyelids, his nose, his lips. He opened his mouth and caught one of the nipples gently, sucking, bringing his hands up to hold, stroke, pinch them.

"Oh, Skye. Oh, *Dios*."

She moaned and rubbed her pubis hard against his swelling desire. Then she fell forward onto him, using her hands to hoist up her skirts. She was panting, writhing. He undid his jeans and pulled them off while her hand sought him.

"Ah," she said, as she found him. "*Grande. Mucho grande.* And this has been worth waiting for." She raised her hips above him and paused. He felt the warmth of her wetness on the very tip. She rotated her hips once, very slowly, moving him just inside her. He thrust upward.

"Ah!" she said, pulling away. "No, no, no." Fargo smiled up at her enjoying the sight of her black shining eyes, her hair falling about them, his hands cupping her hanging breasts.

Again, she moved her hips and paused. Then he felt her contract around him and she lowered herself onto him, inch by inch, squeezing him gently until he was fully inside her. He pulled her face down to him and thrust his tongue into her mouth, and thrust himself deeply upward into her. She began to move on him, rhythmically, contracting, her tongue in his mouth, thrusting with him, deeply, hot and wet. He felt the gathering together and then he grasped her, turning her on her back and gave himself to her again, again, again, his hands wound in her dark hair, until it was black and silent.

He kissed her gently on the eyelids and rolled onto his back beside her, sitting up suddenly. They had not even waited to get out the bedrolls, he realized as the grit stuck to his sweating back. He chuckled.

"You were certainly in a hurry," he said, brushing off his back and chucking her under the chin.

"You, too," she said, lazily stretching. They rose and brushed themselves off, fetched the bedrolls and spread them out. She nestled next to him and he heard her breathing slow toward sleep.

"Antonia?"

"Hm?"

"About the monks."

"The ones who brought the Silver Maria?"

"Yes. What happened to them?"

"*Tragedia*. The conquistadors tortured them to find out where they had hidden the Silver Maria. But they all died rather than tell."

Fargo lay awake for a long time, listening to Antonia's soft breathing beside him, listening to the weird silence of the night, thinking of the Silver Maria.

*   *   *

He came awake in the middle of the night. Something was moving. He sat up silently, saw a large hulking form, and felt for his Colt. Then he relaxed as his eyes adjusted to the darkness.

"Barney?" he called out softly, in order not to alarm Antonia.

Barney grunted. He was on his way back to the spot where he had been sleeping. Fargo lay back down and went to sleep, his hand on the revolver.

Dawn was silent in the Diablo country. Fargo awoke as the east turned pale yellow. He arose and stowed his bedroll. He would have a look around.

He passed by Barney, who lay snoring, a dark stain on the sand before him. Fargo halted. Blood? He took a step forward.

"Goddamn it!" he swore. Barney lay clutching one of the canteens. The cap was off it and the water had leaked out into the sand. He had been thirsty in the middle of the night and had gotten up to find water, Fargo realized. Goddamn.

Fargo leaned down and wrested the canteen from the sleeping man's grip, careful not to spill out any water that might remain. He put the cap on again and sloshed it around. There wasn't much. Maybe a few swallows. And one full canteen. Much less than enough for the three of them.

It was dangerous to go forward with not enough water. They would have to go back. Replenish their water. Damn. And maybe run smack into the regiment.

He returned the canteen to the saddlebag and climbed up the rocks above the overhang, heading for the top of the mesa. It was rough going, he thought as he hauled himself up over a steep ledge. All about him the red rock formations began to show pink in the dawn. Finally, he climbed to the top of the mesa and hauled himself up. He turned to look in the direction of the entrance to the Diablo and Last Chance Water Hole.

He could see the dry mud flat clearly through a gap in the jagged canyon wall. There was a dark movement on the dun-colored plain. Moving figures, flashing even from this distance, horses, men. It could only be the regiment, he realized. Less than a mile behind them.

They couldn't go back. They had to go forward. With a little more than one canteen of water. He would stop drinking water altogether. It had to go for Antonia and Barney. They would have to ride continuously. No more overnight rests. They would have to move out. Fast. Now.

Fargo started down the rocks, scrambling quickly, gravity pulling him. He came to the steep narrow ledge and felt his way along, hugging the rock face and making his way toward the wider flat area just ahead. He rounded the boulder and then stopped. Ahead of him five feet away crouched a mountain lion, yellow eyes wide and focused, muscles tense.

Behind it were three kittens, flattened into a cleft. It was protecting its young. The most dangerous time.

He backed up slowly, scraping against the rock and felt, too late, the holster strapped to his thigh turn upended. He fumbled for the Colt as it slid out of the holster, bounced on the rock ledge, and fell ten feet down the hill, discharging as it landed. The gunshot echoed, amplified by the rocks around them.

Great. Just in case Stalling is wondering which direction we went. And as he thought this, the mountain lion leapt.

6

Skye threw his arms up around his neck to protect his throat and braced himself for the mountain lion's impact, all two hundred pounds. As it struck, he rolled with its weight, feeling teeth sink into his forearm, seeking his neck. Its claws tore at his arms. He was glad for the buckskin jacket he had thrown on before his climb. It gave him some protection.

The cat's back paws clawed him convulsively with its powerful legs. He heard his jeans tear and felt the searing pain on his thighs as they rolled over. He wouldn't last long.

For a moment, he held it by the loose skin on either side of its neck. It writhed and spit, and one of its paws caught his cheek, which burned as the claws scratched his face.

No chance to reach the knife at his ankle. If he let go of it, he might get its teeth in his neck. Couldn't outrun a mountain lion either. But he was close to the edge of the cliff. That was a chance. He could take the fall.

With one hand he let go his grip on its ruff and hit the cat with a hard, uppercut in the belly. The breath left the mountain lion's body and it relaxed for a moment. He rolled away, toward the edge of the ledge and, spreading his arms and legs, he rolled on over it into space.

The fall was only a few feet and his arms and legs snagged the jagged rocks and broke his descent. Nothing broken. Hardly bruised. He came to his feet immediately, bracing himself on the rocks. He looked up. The mountain lion crouched at the edge looking down at him warily, eyes two pinpoints of blackness on discs of wicked yellow. He backed away a few steps and looked about for his Colt. It was further down. He continued to move slowly backward down the slope, watching it. He bent to retrieve the revolver, and when he glanced up, the mountain lion had disappeared.

Skye examined his arm, where the mountain lion's teeth had entered. A clean bite. It would heal. His face stung. He hurried down the hill and reached the overhang. Antonia and Barney were mounted, ready to ride. Antonia's face was relieved as it saw him and then horrified.

"Skye! What happened? The gunshot! And . . ."

He looked down at himself and saw his torn jeans and his bloodstained clothing. He probably looked worse than he felt.

"No time to explain," he said. "Stalling is not far away. And he's heard the same shot. He's heading this way right now. Let's move."

They rode down the slope and turned up the trail, riding hard as they could, then slowing and letting the horses get their wind, then riding them hard again. The morning sun appeared over the canyon wall and then beat down on them. The still air in the deep dry canyon blasted heat like a cruel oven. By late afternoon the sweating Appaloosas were dragging, their mouths foaming with thirst. The pinto was sturdier, but had slowed. They couldn't keep going at this pace.

Just ahead, the trail split, he remembered. The *cañón à la derecha*, right-hand canyon, and *cañón à la izquierda* on the left. They would go left and hole up for a few hours in a blind gorge just ahead, if memory served. The entrance was so narrow, wide enough for only one rider at a time, that one man could defend it, if need be. It could buy them some time. Or, if the regiment tracked them there, it might be a deathtrap. He'd have to take that chance.

Fargo turned the mare onto the left-hand trail. It was tired, hot, and thirsty and not responding well. Barney followed on the Ovaro and Antonia on the Appaloosa stallion.

He scanned the rock face wall of the canyon for the entrance to the hidden gorge and finally rode straight toward what appeared to be a solid wall. As he neared, the rocks seemed to part and he could see the small crevice that he remembered as the entrance. He rode the Appaloosa into it.

It went hesitantly, not liking the rock walls so close to her flanks, and towering far above. They wound through the narrow chasm, the rock sometimes brushing his knees on either side.

They had almost reached the gorge when Fargo heard a sound. He reined in and turned back, signaling Barney and Antonia to remain quiet. There it was again. A clattering of rocks overhead. A small shower of pebbles landed on the path before him. He looked down at them and listened. Silence.

Vultures nesting in the rocks above? More mountain lions? Or something worse. He didn't like it. Every instinct in him told him not to go forward. He turned around and looked again at Antonia and Barney. There wasn't room to turn the horses around and, for a moment, he considered backing the horses through the chasm. His Ovaro could do that. But not two wild Appaloosas. He sighed and listened again. Nothing.

He motioned them forward and, in another moment, they broke out of the rock chasm into the gorge, littered with large boulders. His sharp eyes picked up movement. Movement in the rocks, movement overhead. His Colt revolver was half out of his holster when a deep voice said "Freeze! Drop it."

Fargo kept his hand on his revolver as more than twenty men appeared all around him from behind the rocks. A short dark man with a large mustache, strapped round with several belts of ammunition, sauntered toward him. He held a large carved silver pistol before him, aimed at Fargo's heart. The man smiled very slowly, his eyes flickered from Fargo to Antonia to Barney.

Fargo realized he was looking into the eyes of Reynaldo Reyes.

"Drop it. Now. Señor."

Fargo did as he was told, tossing the Colt onto the ground a few feet away.

"Tres viajeros!" Reyes said. "Three tired travelers in this beautiful land." He began to walk around them slowly as they sat on their horses. Then he whirled about suddenly. "Get down!"

Several of his men came forward immediately and pulled them down from their horses. Fargo stole a glance at Antonia. She had tucked her hair beneath her wide-brimmed hat and had worn the vest he had given her. In her dust-covered clothes, she might pass for a boy. He hoped.

The bandits pushed them roughly into a line and Reyes walked back and forth in front of them, looking at each of them carefully. Some of the men had led their horses from where they had been hidden behind the rocks. Several of the mounts were lame. The horses had been ridden hard and mistreated.

"I do not often see travelers on this trail," said

Reyes. "And with three such horses." He inspected the Appaloosas. Then he stopped before the Ovaro and stroked its neck.

"This one is very fine. A rare pinto. Very strong, intelligent. I can always tell from the eyes." He turned away from the horse, back toward them. "So, señors, you must forgive me if I am overtaken with amazement. And what kind of guests do I have here who have come to my special place uninvited?" He stopped in front of Barney McCann.

"A big man. Very strong." Reyes lifted Barney's hat as he gazed blankly in front of him. "But somebody has been shooting at him." He lowered the hat again. "You talk?" Barney shuffled his feet. Reyes shrugged and turned toward Antonia. If they discovered she was a woman . . .

Fargo held his breath and his eyes flicked over the scene. How many men, how many guns, and where. The nearest rock cover. If he grabbed Antonia and dove for it. All this he calculated in a second and his hopes sank. Not a chance. Not one goddamn chance.

"And what have we here? Very pretty boy." Antonia shuffled as Barney had done and looked down, trying to look like an awkward adolescent. It was convincing.

"Come se llama?" Reyes asked. Antonia glanced at Fargo who shook his head almost imperceptibly. Reyes noticed. "Another silent one? Maybe this one has been shot in the head, too?" He put his hand on the brim of Antonia's hat.

"He just doesn't like strangers," Fargo said. Reyes whirled around.

"I didn't ask you," Reyes said, turning back to Antonia.

"Too stupid, I guess," Fargo said. He saw the men around him draw back and Reyes turned again to him.

"How is that again?" he asked slowly.

"Estupido," Fargo repeated. Reyes advanced toward him and drew his pistol, his hand shaking with rage. Well, he'd drawn Reynaldo's attention away from Antonia. But he might have overplayed a bit. The barrel was one of the old-fashioned ones, very long and about as thick as a cannon, carved elaborately in Mexican silver.

"You are the stupid one," Reyes said. He looked Fargo up and down very slowly, noting the torn jeans and his bloodied thigh, the tear in the forearm of his buckskin jacket, and the scratch along his cheek. Fargo had a sudden inspiration.

"She was very beautiful, but very fierce," he said quietly to Reyes.

Reyes looked up at him and then, very slowly, he smiled, his eyes crinkling at the corners.

"You are going to tell me this was done by a woman?" he said, beginning to laugh. Antonia shifted nervously. "It was a mountain lion, I think."

"No," Fargo said in mock seriousness. He spoke in a loud voice so all of the men could hear him. "I'm sure it was a woman. Listen to my story. I had been on the trail for a month. No women anywhere. I looked all around and someone told me, go to the Diablo country. There are plenty of women there. Women all over the place. Very hot women."

Reyes leaned back and laughed loudly. The men joined him.

"So, I came looking for these women," Fargo continued. "I looked everywhere, but I couldn't find them. Where were these hot devil women? I was getting desperate."

The men continued to laugh, making obscene gestures. Reyes was wiping the tears of laughter from his eyes. It wasn't that funny, Fargo thought, but he was glad the audience was getting such a kick out of it.

"Finally, this morning I was climbing up the mesa and I saw her. The devil woman! Just like they said. With beautiful big yellow eyes. Freckled from the sun. Beautifully muscled legs. And very narrow in the hips." Fargo outlined the shape of narrow hips with his hands and the men whistled. "And when she turned around, oh, the most beautiful tail in the world."

The men were going crazy, some of them panto-miming mountain lions and other men pumping their hips.

"Oh, if I had a woman right now, I would give it to her," one of them shouted. Fargo saw Antonia jam her hands into her jeans pockets. Probably to hide their shaking, he thought.

"So," Fargo continued, "I said 'Devil woman, I have come to make love to you.' And she must have been eager because she jumped right on me!"

Reyes slapped his thigh and hooted.

"And . . . she . . . scratched?" he said, gasping for breath.

"The better the man, the more the women scratch. And bite too," Fargo said. "Would you like me to tell you where I found her? She would like to scratch and bite a man as famous as Reynaldo Reyes."

At the sound of his name, Reyes became sober again. A few of the men continued to horse around and were quickly shushed by the others.

"So. You know my name. I do not know yours."

"Skye Fargo. Some people call me the The Trailsman."

Reyes's face remained impassive. If he recognized Fargo's name, he did not show it. He would be a good poker partner, Fargo thought. Well, maybe another day.

"An interesting name," Reyes said. "And why is Señor Fargo in the Diablo country?" Fargo thought fast.

"I am trying to catch up with an Army regiment on their way through the Diablo. They have a lot of extra horses—good fast horses—and I was hoping to buy some."

Reyes's eyebrows shot up and his glinting dark eyes searched Fargo's face. He wasn't that good a poker player, Fargo decided.

"Go through their bags," Reyes said.

Fargo hoped Antonia had stored the map in her blouse again and not in the saddlebags. He dared not look in her direction. The bandits rifled through the bags and came forward with the two canteens.

"This is all?" Reyes said, unscrewing the cap of the full one and taking a long drink. He passed it back to the man who had handed it to him. The man drank and passed it on. Fargo saw the other canteen emptied by two men and then thrown down on the ground.

A piercing whistle sounded above them. They all looked up. On the top of the gorge wall stood one of Reyes's men. He was gesturing wildly and pointing toward the canyon which lay beyond the narrow entranceway.

"The regiment," Fargo guessed.

"With horses," Reyes said, almost to himself. "Well, I would like to stay and hear more women stories, but we must go. Thank you for bringing us the fresh horses, señor."

Goddamn it. Reyes was going to take their three horses—including the Ovaro. Fargo sized up the group again. His Colt revolver was now in the hands of one of the bandits. There were about twenty of them. One of him. Son of a bitch. This had been a helluva day. So far.

Reyes strode quickly forward and seized the reins of the Ovaro. The horse snorted. He pulled the bridle down hard and tried to mount. The pinto sidestepped and Reyes stumbled. He seized the bridle of the nearest Appaloosa and mounted.

"Bring that pinto along," he said. He looked down at the three of them standing there. "And bring the boy. He would be useful to us." Two of the men stepped toward Antonia and Fargo tensed, reviewed the odds again, looking for a way. Reyes turned back.

"On second thought, leave him. He looks soft. A soft boy is a lot of trouble. Give me the señor's pistol." The Colt revolver was handed up to Reyes. He held it in his hand. "This gun has seen many men die," he said thoughtfully. He unlocked the chamber and looked inside, removing some of the bullets.

"At least leave us the gun," Fargo said.

"Señor Fargo, I am a merciful man," Reyes said. "Anyone will tell you that. So, I will leave you the gun with three bullets. Why three? Can anyone guess?" He looked around at his men, who shook their heads. They were a tough bunch of *hombres*, Fargo thought, but they were all obviously afraid of Reynaldo Reyes.

"So we can put ourselves out of our misery," Fargo said.

"Exactly," Reyes said. "Not that I would wish such a thing. A man who can tell such women stories deserves to live. So, I will leave the gun at the entrance to the gorge as we leave. You can pick it up on your way out. You have about as much chance of surviving the Diablo as you do of . . . of finding the Silver Maria!" He laughed as he rode off.

The bandits mounted quickly and rode out in single file through the chasm. Fargo watched as one on horseback tugged at the pinto's bridle and another following whipped the horse from behind. The Ovaro was reluctant to leave and balked and reared, but they finally forced it into the chasm. Fargo stood looking after them for a long, long time in the silence. Goddamn.

No water. A gun with three bullets. That is, if Reyes left it as he said he would. And two long day's ride to water. And no horses. Fargo thought about the Ovaro being led through the chasm. Damn. The faithful pinto had been with him for a long time.

He turned and looked at Antonia and Barney standing beside him. The large man was staring after the bandits.

"Osses. On," Barney said.

"Yes, Barney," Antonia said. "The horses are gone. That bastard, *hijo di puta!*" Fargo saw her jaw tighten. But no tears.

"Okay," he said. "Let's look around. Pick up anything they've left behind. No matter what. It might help us survive."

In a few minutes they reassembled. Fargo had found six empty cartridge shells. Antonia had picked up some twine and one of their canteens which had been emptied and discarded. And Barney found a strip of canvas, ripped off a saddlebag.

"Not bad," Fargo said. He screwed the cap on the canteen and handed it to Antonia. "There may be a little left. Try it when you can't hold out any longer." She slung the canteen over her shoulder.

"What will we do now?" Antonia asked.

"With Last Chance dried up, water's two days back," Fargo said. "Of course, that's riding. Walking will take us three or four days."

"And ahead?" Antonia said.

"About the same distance. Maybe a little more," he said thoughtfully.

"I say go forward," Antonia said. "Every step brings us closer to the heart of the country."

Fargo looked at her and at Barney. Backward or forward, it was about the same difference. Their chances of getting through the Diablo alive were about as bad as they could get. On foot with no water. But it was the same distance back. They might as well go forward. He nodded.

"We'll set off now and walk through the night," he said. "During the heat of the day, we'll rest in the shade." He kept the rest to himself.

He led them out of the chasm. By the entrance he found the Colt revolver with three bullets in the chamber. He looked across the empty canyon at the lengthening shadows. The sun was nearly set. No sign of the regiment or of the Reyes gang.

Fargo set a rapid and steady pace across the canyon floor, looking back from time to time to see how Antonia and Barney were keeping up. His thoughts were running far away on the trail, with the black-and-white pinto. Goddamn Reyes.

They walked through the nightfall. He called a halt when they had gone about ten miles. They had reached the top of No-Name Pass, a rocky defile leading from one canyon to another.

"Wait here," he said to Barney and Antonia. It was hard to speak the words. His dry tongue didn't move easily in his mouth. They sat down immediately on the rocks, too tired to answer. Fargo had seen some slopes on the backside of the pass, as they had climbed up the trail. He scrambled up the rocks and over the top and found what he was looking for.

In the moonlight he saw a patch of rocky soil and the low lumps of cactus here and there. Fishhook barrel cactus, he saw. Not the juciest kind, but it would have to do. And not big either. The size of two fists at the biggest. He stripped off his buckskin jacket and dropped it over one, wrenching it from the earth. He gathered ten more of them, the largest of those on the slope, and returned to Antonia and Barney.

He still had the knife strapped around his ankle. He pulled it out and sliced open the cactus. He gave them pieces of the cactus and showed them how to hold the slices inside their hats and bury their faces in it to suck out the little bit of bitter juice. They didn't talk. After a while, he rose and motioned for them to follow. They set off again.

They were half a mile away before he realized they had left the pieces of cactus on the rocks beside the trail. For a moment, he considered returning to hide them. Oh hell, he thought. If the regiment caught up with them, at least they'd get a drink of water. He was tired, he realized. And thirsty. Leaving the cactus rinds by the trail had been a mistake. He couldn't afford to make mistakes.

Two hours later, walking by the light of the moon, they came upon a carcass beside the trail. The peccary had been dead for only a day or two. Its bones were stripped of most of the meat. Tatters of its bristly skin lay about the skeleton. Fargo knelt down and inspected it carefully.

"What is it?" said Antonia.

"Nothing," Fargo muttered, hastening on. The head of the wild pig had been turned in a peculiar way to face the east. The feet were lined up carefully toward the south. Apaches did that as a sign of thanks to the hunting god. That's what they did with animals. With men, they took scalps.

At the first sign of light in the east, Fargo called a halt at the edge of a sand flat, surrounded by rock formations. They would rest in the rock shadows during the heat of the day. Barney McCann had been shuffling the last few miles and muttering wordlessly to himself. Antonia had been silent but he saw that her eyes were dull and her lips were cracked and bleeding. He pointed to where they would rest and Antonia and Barney threw themselves down on the ground.

Fargo looked around. Nothing moving. No signs of cactus. No grass or leaves to chew on. His mouth was dust dry and his eyes smarted. All he wanted was water. And rest.

Fargo unrolled the piece of canvas that Barney had found. Using the knife, he quickly dug a hole in the still cool earth. Then he spread the canvas over it. The heat of the morning would bring any moisture in the cool soil up to the surface. It would only be a drop or two. But it would be something. Then he lay down close to the rock which would shade him. He dreamed of water. Cool water.

He awoke in midmorning as the day began to heat up. He remembered the canvas and hastened to look, pulling up a corner. The underside was covered with droplets of water. He carefully raised the canvas and then, holding an edge of it curled under to catch the droplets, he flipped it. The water ran to the middle of the cupped canvas. A swallow. Or two.

He took it over to Antonia and woke her gently. She took a small sip. She nodded, her eyes saying thanks. He realized it was difficult for her to speak with her lips swollen and dried. He woke Barney, who took the rest of the water and then looked up at Fargo as if to ask why there wasn't more. Skye rose and went back to his resting place. He lay down and put the barely moist canvas over his face and dreamed.

It was midafternoon before he awoke again, feeling stronger. He could feel his tongue swelling in his mouth. It made him less thirsty. He looked about. Antonia was sleeping. Barney was gone. Fargo rose and looked all about him. Away across the sand flat, half a mile away, he saw the staggering figure of a man walking, silhouetted against the shimmering silver of the reflected sun, which made the sand flat look like a cool lake. That was it. Barney thought he was walking toward water. Cursing, Fargo set out after him.

On the smooth sand, he saw the sinuous curving tracks of a sidewinder rattlesnake. The Diablo was swarming with rattlesnakes. He would warn Antonia about them when they got back. He caught up with Barney in a few minutes.

"McCann!" he said sharply. "There's no water out here. Come back." The lumbering man turned to look at him.

"Wa," he said, pointing toward the mirage, which receded before them, never to be reached.

"No," Fargo said. He took his arm and pulled him back toward the shelter of the rocks. He'd have to keep an eye on Barney. He was unpredictable. It wasn't Barney's fault. But it could get them all killed.

Antonia was stirring when they returned. The sun was low and soon it would be time to walk again. Fargo sat down again and Barney sat beside him.

"Where were you?" Antonia asked, sitting up. She removed her shoes and began to rub her sore feet.

"Barney wandered off," he answered. "We'll have to keep an eye on him."

Antonia nodded and rose, walking gingerly over the rough sand and gravel, looking about. Fargo rested his head against the rock and closed his eyes. A moment later he heard her scream. He leapt to his feet and found her on the other side of a small outcropping, standing stock still, her face pale, eyes wide.

"Serpiente de cascabel! My foot!"

The sidewinder rattlesnake was looping its way away from her across the sand.

"Don't move," he commanded. In a stride, he caught up to the snake, seized it by the tail, swung it over his head and dashed its head against the rocks.

"Sit down," he told Antonia. "Make as little motion as possible." The two puncture wounds on her foot were already swelling with poison. He pulled the twine out of his pocket and tied it tightly around her shin, then pulled the knife from his ankle holster. She looked away as he took her foot and made the first cut. She didn't flinch, but he saw her hands dig into the gravel. He made the second cut crosswise.

Then he put his mouth over the cross and sucked. He was so thirsty, he had to fight the temptation to swallow her blood tainted with the snake's poison. He spit it out and sucked on the wound again and again. After a few minutes, he was sure he had it all.

Antonia lay quietly, her face drawn. Except for her scream, she hadn't made another noise. A remarkable woman, Fargo thought. He loosened the twine and gently rubbed her leg to restore the circulation. What little poison might be left would make her a little weak, but it wouldn't kill her.

"It's okay," he said. "You're going to be all right." She sat up and nestled against him. He saw her chin quiver and the tears starting in her eyes. She blinked to fight them back.

"I was very frightened," she said. He held her close for a while in silence. It would be hard for her to walk through the long night, he realized. Once again he wondered where the Ovaro was. Damn Reyes. Just for the hell of it, he whistled. It took several tries, because his lips were so dry, but finally he managed it. He listened, hoping for the sound of hoofbeats. He whistled again. Antonia looked up at him.

"Will we make it?" she asked.

"Sure," he said. "Sure." He wished he felt as certain as he sounded. "That's our dinner that bit you. Let's eat."

He chopped the rattlesnake into three portions, carefully carving away its poison glands. Skye slit the pieces lengthwise and took the thinner tail for himself and handed the fleshier parts to Antonia and Barney. There was no point in lighting a fire and cooking it. They needed what little juices it had. He showed them how to suck on the raw snake and pick its flesh from the bones.

Raw rattlesnake had never been his favorite dish, he thought as he picked a bone splinter out of his teeth. But it was better than nothing. And who knew when they would find anything else?

"Isn't this delicious?" he said to Antonia. She was having a hard time of it, sucking and then gagging. Barney didn't seem to mind at all.

"*Bueno*," she said grimly. "*Mucho bueno*." He grinned and she smiled back. What a helluva mess, he thought.

At sundown, they moved on. They were across the sand flat in an hour and walking up a rugged canyon. Antonia's foot was worse than he had anticipated. She was limping badly. He slowed the pace, but still he could tell she was struggling. Finally he stopped.

"Natonee hut," Barney said.

"Yes. She's hurt," Fargo answered him. "Let me see your foot." She pulled up her skirt and showed him how she had unlaced her boot. The foot had swollen to twice its size. She needed rest. Or at least not to be walking on it.

"Get on my back," he said.

"Skye, you can't carry me through the Diablo!"

"Try it," he said. "At least for now." He bent over as she wrapped her arms about his neck and her legs around his waist. Luckily, she was not a heavy woman, he thought as he straightened up. It would be rough going, but they would make better time if he carried her.

They plodded on for another three hours until it was close to midnight. Sometimes when things were bad, Fargo thought, a sudden piece of good luck would happen. A water hole. A field of barrel cactus. A wandering pony. Or three. He put the thoughts out of his mind quickly.

Then he concentrated on how they would make it. After tonight, it would be two nights more. Two nights more of hard going. Three at the most. If he could find just a little more for them to eat. More cactus. Just a couple. And if there happened to be some water. Or some ponies. Dammit! There he went again.

He closed his thoughts off and kept his mind a blank, his eyes constantly scanning the terrain, his ears alert to the silence of the desert night, putting his strength into his legs, keeping them climbing the rocks, marching on the trail.

He thought about the black-and-white Ovaro. Where was it now? Was Reyes mistreating it? How would he find his faithful pinto again? He imagined the horses's strong chest and rippling muscles, his lean haunches and beautiful coat. The intelligence of his eyes. He remembered the feel of the pinto beneath him, the hoofbeats on the trail, and it was as if, in the distance, he could hear the Ovaro's hooves. Hear them pounding, riding hard. Many horses riding hard. He shook his head.

"Get down," he said to Antonia. He knelt immediately and put his ear to the ground. Yes, horses galloping. The sound was far away but getting louder. Who would be riding in the middle of the night. Reyes again? The regiment? Apaches?

He looked about them. They couldn't be in a worse position, trapped in a narrow canyon with few places to hide. One chance, he thought. He scanned the steep rock walls lit by the moonlight and saw a crumbling section that would give them an easy climbing route to the top.

"Horses coming. Don't know who. We're climbing up," he told them.

In minutes the horses would be here. If they made it to the top of the mesa, they'd be safe. And even if they were far up on the rocks, hidden in the shadows, the riders might not see them. They would have to hurry.

"I can climb," Antonia insisted. The three of them began to scramble up the jagged rocks. Barney was clumsy and slow.

"Faster," Skye said. "C'mon." They were only three-quarters of the way up the rocks when he heard the hoofbeats approaching, coming closer. "Stay still," he ordered them. "Get back in the shadows. Don't move."

Down below, the riders came into view galloping up the trail, distinct in the moonlight. It was the regiment. Fargo noted that there were only a dozen of them. There had been about twenty. Had they split up? Or had they run into the Reyes gang?

The regiment was being led by the Tonto Apache scout. Fargo held his breath. He saw the tall figure of Fox Stalling and he cursed inwardly. Just keep going, he said to them silently. But the Apache scout raised his hand and the regiment halted.

The Indian rode forward a few paces and sat tall on

his mount. Fargo could see him looking from side to side and all about the canyon as he shrank back into the shadow. Ride on, he said to them silently.

He watched as Fox Stalling rode up to the scout. They conferred for a moment.

"Hey, Fargo!" Stalling shouted. "We know you're here! Give it up. You'll never make it!"

Skye glanced at Antonia and Barney. They were well hidden in shadowy crevices. If they just waited long enough, the Indian might think he was wrong and they would move on.

"C'mon, Antonia!" Stalling shouted. "We've been tracking you. You're on foot. You'll never make it!"

There was a silence and then the ponies shifted under the men, spurs clinked, saddles creaked. Fargo waited.

"Hey, Barney! Barney McCann!" Stalling called. "You want some water? I got some nice cool water for you!"

At the sound of his name, Barney started. His foot slipped on the rocks and a tumble of stones clattered noisily down the hillside.

7

The men of the regiment looked up immediately in the direction of the falling rocks. Fargo cursed.

"Come on," he said to Antonia and Barney. "Our only chance is to get to the top of this mesa and make a run for it." He began scrambling up the boulders again, glancing behind him from time to time. Antonia was struggling on her bad foot. Barney was clumsy. It was slow going.

He looked down to the floor of the canyon. The regiment was dividing up, half the men advancing to the foot of the rockslide. Four men and Fox Stalling rode off down the trail, led by the Apache scout. Damn. There must be another way around to the top of the mesa.

"Come on, dammit!" he said. The summit was not far away. The men down below were not bothering to climb up after them, but sat silently on their mounts watching. With a final burst of energy, Fargo climbed the last few boulders and hauled himself onto the top of the mesa.

Before him, the flat tabletop spread out, punctuated by low irregular mounds of rocks, which seemed to waver in the pale moonlight. The mesa was long and narrow. One end curved and descended, a natural pathway. He guessed the regiment would be riding up there any moment. In the distance, the other end narrowed to a precarious bridge and joined another mesa to the south. They would have to run in that direction. He turned and watched as Antonia and Barney climbed the last few feet, and he bent down to help them up.

"No time to waste," he said. "Get on my back, Antonia. Let's go."

Fargo and Barney half walked and half ran across the weird landscape between the mounds of rocks. They had gone some distance before Fargo realized the mounds were man-made. Then he knew what they were. They were walking through an Apache graveyard.

A large mound of stones was ahead of them. On the cairn lay a body. An Apache chief from the looks of him—silverwork across his chest, silver bracelets. Fargo saw Barney slow down.

"Don't stop, Barney," Fargo said. "We must hurry."

The big man did not seem to hear and he paused beside the cairn, looking down at the Apache chief.

"Ed. Cohnel Delgado ed."

"Yes, Barney," Antonia snapped, still on Fargo's back. "Colonel Delgado is dead. Come now."

"Iver," Barney said, reaching out to touch the ornaments on the Apache's body.

"Don't!" Fargo said. "Goddamn it, McCann!" Barney began to stroke the ornaments, then bent down and put his head on the dead Indian's chest.

Fargo let Antonia slip down off his back and approached Barney.

"Get off that!" he said roughly, seizing Barney's arm.

"Iver. Must fine. Iver Maria. For Cohnel Delgado."

"Yes, Barney," Antonia shouted at him. "We'll find the Silver Maria. We'll find it for Julio. But come on. Now!"

Fargo pulled at him, but Barney clung to the dead body, as if it were Julio Delgado. Skye pulled harder and the corpse began to slide off the rocks. Shit, he thought. He looked around, but nothing moved on the top of the mesa. Apaches always guarded their recent dead which lay in state until they were buried. Any moment, the three of them might have arrows in their backs.

"Let go!" he said and punched Barney in the gut. He heard the sound of hoofbeats. Barney staggered backward, releasing his hold on the Indian. Then he came straight at Fargo.

"Barney, no!" Antonia said. But he hit Fargo with all his fury, and the two of them rolled to the ground, punching. Barney was fighting with all the anger that had been pent-up since the terrible incident in the sand pit, Fargo realized as he dodged his blows. He didn't want to hurt Barney, but they didn't have time to be rolling around while the regiment caught up with them.

Fargo hit him in his soft belly, taking the wind out of him and then gave him a swift uppercut in the jaw. McCann's head flew back and his eyes rolled in his head. He turned over and lay still. Fargo heard the noise of jangling saddles and spurs all around him.

He got shakily to his feet, his head reeling. He felt the tiredness, the thirst, the lack of food, the cougar's scratches and bites still aching.

"Well, well. What have we here?" Fox Stalling said, looking down at Fargo from atop his horse. One of his men had already dismounted and held Antonia, who was struggling. Fargo looked about. Four men plus Stalling. The Apache scout was nowhere in sight. Fargo guessed that the Indian was willing to betray his people, but not to trespass into the graveyard.

"Fancy meeting you here," Fargo said.

"You're a little the worse for wear, Mr. Fargo," Stalling replied. "And traveling by foot! Where are the fine horses that we tracked?" There was no reason not to tell him, Fargo thought.

"Somebody took a fancy to them," Fargo answered. He heard the bitterness in his words at the thought of the Ovaro in the hands of those bandits. "Somebody by the name of Reynaldo Reyes."

"That bastard!" Stalling said, at the mention of Reyes. Fargo smiled to himself, remembering the boast the major had made about taking care of the Reyes gang once and for all.

"And, where are the rest of your fine men?" Fargo asked. "You're missing some."

"Shut up!" Stalling snapped. So, the regiment had tangled with Reynaldo, Fargo thought. And it hadn't been a victory.

Before Stalling collected himself he had to act, Fargo realized. His eyes flicked over Stalling and the four men as he calculated his chances. He had three bullets. One was for Stalling. For sure. And if he took out two other men, that would leave two. He might be able to hold off two. All the men had guns. Two with them drawn. One holding Antonia.

In a flash Fargo drew his Colt. Stalling first. He fired and just at that moment, the major's mount shifted. The shot caught Stalling in the shoulder, knocking him half out of his saddle.

Fargo dived for the ground as a shot whizzed by him, rolling and coming up on one knee to shoot at the skinny soldier who had fired. The bullet hit dead center in the gut and the man slumped to the ground. His pistol discharged as he fell, the shot flying wide. But Fargo had already spun about to take care of the third soldier, who was covering him, pistol drawn. Fargo blasted the revolver out of his grip and the man yelped with pain, grabbing his gun hand with the other. Fargo wheeled about as the fourth man drew.

"Drop it," Skye said, holding the Colt revolver before him. He had spent the three bullets. All he had.

His gun was now empty. But if he played his cards right, they might not find out.

The private, a towheaded kid, hesitated.

"I said drop it," Fargo repeated. The kid started to obey.

"No, you drop it," Fargo heard. He turned. The soldier holding Antonia had quietly drawn his knife and held it against her throat.

"That's right, goddamn you," Stalling said. He had rolled down off his horse and stood, cradling his arm, his gun hand. His shattered shoulder oozed blood. "Drop it, Fargo. We got 'cha outnumbered. Who you going to shoot first?"

Fargo turned toward Stalling. The major couldn't draw his gun because his holster was on the side of his wounded shoulder. What he would give for one more bullet for Stalling, Fargo thought grimly. But he would see how far Stalling would go.

Fargo raised the Colt up to eye level, taking careful aim at a point just between Stalling's eyes. On one side he heard the click of the soldier's pistol, pointed straight at him.

"Shoot me and my gun goes off," Fargo said. "Right between the major's eyes. Let go of Antonia." Stalling was sweating. Fargo could see the wet sheen on his face even in the dim moonlight. Who would give in first? A long moment passed. Fargo felt the exhaustion, hunger, and thirst which made him feel hollow, light-headed. He gripped the Colt firmly, but it wavered. Stalling's eyes shifted to the gun aimed at his forehead and then he looked back into Fargo's eyes. Stalling's eyes narrowed.

"Slice her neck," said Stalling coolly.

Antonia screamed. Fargo threw down his empty Colt and glanced at Antonia. She was holding her throat. Blood seeped between her fingers. She pulled her hand away. No gushing, Fargo saw with relief. The artery wasn't severed. Only a surface wound. Stalling advanced on Fargo.

"That was easy," Stalling said. "Hold him, boys." Two of the soldiers came over and held Fargo, one on each side.

"You've been meddling in my business long enough, Fargo." Stalling bent over and retrieved Fargo's Colt with his good hand, fumbling to hold it. He came up close, breathing into Skye's face.

"This is going to give me real pleasure, Mr. Fargo," Stalling said. "I'm going to shoot you with your own gun." Stalling laughed and held the pistol, wavering, before him and squeezed the trigger.

The empty click resounded in the silence. Stalling glared at the gun and pulled the trigger twice more.

"Son of a bitch!" he yelled. He threw down the pistol. "You're gonna regret getting mixed up in this, Fargo," Stalling said. "But not for long. Because you're not going to live much longer."

Stalling drew back his good arm and delivered a hard blow to Fargo's belly. Fargo felt the explosion of pain and the breath left him and the men holding him tightened their grips. He gasped, struggling for air as Stalling stepped back and swung sideways, catching Fargo's jaw. His head bounced painfully to the right and he heard the snap of his neck. Stalling hit him again and again, one way and then the other. The world was a whirling mass of colored darkness, lit by stars, wheeling, and the fist descending again, again. Stalling clubbed him low down and searing pain radiated from between Fargo's legs. He felt his knees give way.

"Let him go," he heard Stalling say. Suddenly he was falling and then he tasted the dust under him and the silvery warmth of his own blood filling his mouth.

Far away, he felt the dull ache of blows, on his back. Rolled over. In his ribs, kicking. The sound of ribs cracking, breaking. A woman's screams. Begging, she was begging for something, promising something.

Someone was laughing. A horse was neighing. He thought of the black-and-white Ovaro, somewhere in the distance, running somewhere in the far-off distance, hoofbeats going away. They were leaving. The world turned under him. Where was he?

He struggled to lift his eyes open. Heaviness and coldness. Rest. Still. That was all he wanted. Rest. Still. But no, open his eyes. He felt the coldness creep along his limbs. Where were his arms and legs? He was only his thoughts now, his body gone. He pushed again and his eyes blinked open. The moonlight shone silver on the rocks. The body of a dead Apache chief flashed silver in the darkness, lying askew on the silver rocks. Silver. Somewhere was silver and a woman, a woman who . . . He couldn't remember.

Even thoughts were being stilled by the creeping cold. He was dying, he knew. He clutched at his anger. Not now. Not now. The cold drew him again. He felt himself rising, being lifted up, up. It grew colder.

Smoke. It burned inside his nostrils. The smoke of burning cedar and sage. He drew it into himself and it burned his lungs. He contracted in a cough and felt the pain stab his chest, shoot fire along his limbs. The pain brought back the darkness.

The acrid hot liquid burned his lip. Yes, he felt it. He pushed against the hard edge resting on his mouth. More hot, burning. He pushed his tongue forward between his lips and touched the edge of the hardness. The liquid spilled into his mouth, hot, burn. Yes, he felt this. He felt the heat, tasted the liquid.

The cup was taken away and Fargo opened his heavy eyelids. A square of light floated high overhead in the blackness. He blinked, concentrating on the light. Where was he?

He stretched, testing his body, his muscles, exploring the soreness of his chest, arms, and legs. He was warm, wrapped under heavy rough blankets. The sharp odor of old smoke was in the air.

Fargo moved his hand to his head and felt the bandages over his skull and face. He felt under the blankets along his side. His ribs had been wrapped, bound in some kind of cotton material. He reached down further. His knees, too, and his shins were all bound tightly. He pressed against the fabric and winced with pain from bruises underneath. His knife and ankle strap were gone.

His eyes had adjusted to the darkness and he saw a face looming, lit dimly by the light falling from above. He made a sudden movement to sit up, but firm hands pushed him down.

"Where am I?" he asked, his words blurred by the constricting bandages around his jaw. He saw the face a little more clearly now, the black shining eyes, the long hair, and smooth cheeks of a woman. "Where am I?" he repeated.

She spoke and he realized she was Indian. What the hell? He started up, and throbbing pain exploded in his head, neck, chest. He fell back into blackness.

The square of light had gone. But the red glow of embers dappled the mud ceiling and walls. Fargo groaned. The face reappeared above him. She loosened the bandages around his face. He tried a smile. She lifted a cup to his lips.

The bitter hot liquid had gone and in its place was a fragrant broth. He sucked it greedily, feeling the

116

hunger in him as the warmth spread inside. He grunted when he had drained the cup.

She spoke again. He tried to make out the words, but it was an Apache dialect he didn't understand. He studied her face. Round cheeks, smooth in the firelight, deep black glittering eyes and braided hair. She smiled back at him, noticing his attention. Then she disappeared.

He remembered the graveyard and the beating. Stalling and his men had just about done him in, he thought ruefully. And now, as far as he could tell, the Apaches had picked him up. But what would they do with him?

Fargo turned onto his side. It was a slow and painful process. He glanced about. He was lying on the floor of a small room with square adobe walls. The light he had seen above him had come from a square window cut in the ceiling to let in the daylight. It was night now, he saw. No light from above. No stars. He wondered about that. A cloudy night in the desert?

Then it struck him. He tried to sit up again. A wave of dizziness swept over him and he clenched his fists to steady himself. Hell. The Apache had picked him up. And they had brought him back to their mountain hideout in the ancient pueblos.

The reason he couldn't see the stars was because the pueblos were built under a gigantic rock ledge. The old pueblos were hard to find and easy to defend. The Apache protected their secret hideouts with all their cunning. So why would they bring a white man into this one? Fargo's head reeled again. He sank back and slept some more.

Daylight again. His face felt better. Some more of the bandages had been removed. Fargo sat up with difficulty and watched as the woman bustled about the

117

small room, folding blankets, stoking the small fire, stirring something in a pot. Her face had been above him every time he had awakened. Day or night. A beautiful face, shy sometimes. Other times with a humorous twinkle.

She moved as gracefully as a deer now, her slim body wrapped closely in the fringed and beaded dress. She looked over and smiled at him, her eyes merry.

Again she spoke. It seemed to be a question. He shook his head. He didn't understand. She pointed to the pot. Fargo grinned and nodded, rubbing his stomach. Yes, he was hungry.

He watched as she ladled something into a pottery bowl and brought it to him. As he slurped the thick stew, he studied her face over the rim of the bowl and wondered what the Apache intended to do with him.

He had seen no one except the woman in the timeless time since he had been brought here. Always her face when he awakened. She had never left him, never seemed to sleep. How had that been possible? He had the sense that time had passed. How many days had it been? Fargo finished the stew and handed the bowl back to her.

"More?" he asked, nodding toward the pot by the fire.

She brought him a second bowl which he ate quickly. The food made him stronger. He should try to get up, he thought. He pushed aside the blankets.

"Got to walk," Fargo said. She shook her head, motioning him to lie back down. He shook his head and willed his legs to move. They bent slowly. He pushed himself up to his knees and tried to stand. The dizziness came back. He was worse off than he had imagined. He bit his lip and pushed again, coming to his knees and then to his feet where he stood swaying.

The woman gave a cry and he reached out and

steadied himself against her. He took a few stumbling steps toward the low entrance, then lurched toward it, grasping the edge of the entry to hold himself steady. He looked out.

In the distance were the sere canyonlands framed above by the broad, smooth lips of a gigantic cave. He felt as if he were looking out from inside the mouth of a mammoth fish. Below him was a wooden ladder leading down from the entrance of the pueblo. There were dozens of the abode boxes built against the back wall of the shallow cave. The ladder led to a flat shelf which dropped off in a precipitous cliff. He looked to the right and saw a narrow rocky path led off to one side. Two sentries stood at the lip of the cave. Escape would be impossible, he thought. Especially in his condition.

Before him on the shelf were Apache women cooking at small fires, grinding grain with the stone mano and matate, weaving baskets of grasses. A yellow puppy chased four children.

Off to the side an old man in a wide cotton headband and flowing white hair sat cross-legged, making arrows. The old man glanced up at the pueblos and saw Fargo standing in the entryway. He shaded his eyes and looked again for a long time. Fargo held up his hand in greeting. The old man dropped the hand shading his eyes and looked down again at his arrows.

Fargo stood watching for a few minutes more, then felt the exhaustion return. He was very weak. Dammit. He turned away; the woman helped him back to the nest of blankets. He fell heavily onto them.

It was night again when he awoke. The woman was there, by the fire. It felt like the middle of the night.

"Don't you ever sleep?" he asked her. She looked up at the sound of his voice and then looked down at the ground, shyly. She hadn't been at all shy that morning, he thought. She brought him two bowls and he ate again. Sweet berries and a hot fragrant liquid, like flower tea.

Afterward, Fargo hauled himself up. It wasn't as hard this time, he thought with satisfaction. He motioned her to come near and, leaning on her, walked again to the entry. The cliff shelf was deserted in the moonlight, the windows of the pueblos dark. He peered at the trail for long moments and saw the shapes of the sentries huddled on the rock saddle. Across the canyonlands, the moon was setting. It was a quarter full and waning.

"Goddamn it," he said softly. Two weeks had passed since he had been here. It had been almost three weeks since he had been with Antonia at Loyal Gulch and she had told him about the Mission Ascension. They only had until the new moon to find the Silver Maria and save the mission. Just over one week to go.

And where was Antonia? And Barney? Fargo thought of the sound of Stalling's laughter as he beat and kicked him. A black rage welled up inside. He thought again of Julio Delgado in the sand pit. Of Padre Ernesto lying dead beside the trail. If Stalling had harmed Antonia . . . or Barney. But here he was, held by Apache and barely able to walk. And time was passing. Fargo pounded the wall in frustration and heard the woman speak beside him.

"I've got to get out of here," he said, looking down at her. She looked up at him in the moonlight and nodded, catching the seriousness of his tone, but not understanding his words. Then she looked away again, suddenly shy.

She was less shy in the morning when he awoke.

"Where's my breakfast?" he asked her. She giggled

as she built up the fire and brought him hot maize in a bowl. After breakfast she brought him a basin of hot water and he washed up. Then she unwound his bandages, replacing some and leaving others off. It was slow and painful work, but she was patient. Finally, she unwound the bandages around his ribs. As the last bit of fabric came off, she tickled his ribs.

Fargo laughed and felt a slight ache. "Hey, don't fool with the patient," he said, reaching for her. She giggled and slid away out of reach. Afterward, Fargo rose again, walked back and forth across the dirt floor, again and again, feeling the stiffness and the bruises of his ordeal. He was feeling stronger by the hour. By the next day, he was sure he could try going down the ladder.

That night she was there again when he awoke in the dark, hungry. Again she fed him and he walked to the entrance and looked out at the night. She looked up at him, the moonlight brushing her smooth skin, and he touched her gently on the cheek, running his finger along her lips. She smiled up at him and then glanced down quickly.

In the morning she woke him for breakfast and washing, all done very hurriedly. Something was up. He was surprised when she motioned him to get to his feet.

"You encouraging me to walk now?" he asked. She motioned him again and he got up, surprised at how much progress he was making. He put his arm over her shoulders and she walked with him through the entrance and out onto the narrow ledge. Below him, the activity of the women and children had ceased. They were all looking up at him, watching.

"Down the ladder?" he said. "Well, this is my lucky day."

He turned around and grasped the poles of the ladder and climbed down slowly. His ribs and legs still ached, but if he moved slowly it was tolerable. He reached the ground and waited for her.

They came from nowhere. Suddenly, as if they materialized out of thin air, Apache braves surrounded him. They encircled him, watching him steadily with their deep black eyes, dressed in yellow-dyed buckskin and blue-and-white pony-beaded leggings. Then one of them, a tall warrior with yellow hail spots painted on his deerskin shirt, nodded toward a ladder which poked out of a round hole nearby. Fargo moved toward it, surrounded by the men.

At their signal, he climbed down into the darkness. When he reached the bottom, he felt firm hands seize him and guide him away from the ladder and push him to the ground. He sat and looked around, hoping his eyes would adjust quickly to the darkness as the other men followed him down the ladder.

He could make out a large, round, windowless room. The only light came from the round hole overhead where the ladder came in. It was hard to see anything.

The last man climbing down the ladder carried a flaming brand between his teeth. He alighted and touched it to a pile of twigs and logs. The fire crackled and caught and Fargo looked about as the sacred kiva lit up with the firelight.

There were many Apache crowded into the room, sitting in rows against the wall. Several of them held sticks with dead birds and feathers tied to the ends. More stuffed birds dangled on cords attached to the high ceiling.

Close to Fargo and in front of the fire sat the white-haired man Fargo had seen before. The old man lifted something to his lips and a piercing whistle sounded, wavered, then stopped.

The old man began to chant. Fargo studied him

carefully. He wore an elaborate three-tiered necklace made of colored beads and slender white bones. Fargo recognized the distinctive shape of human finger bones. What would they do with him?

Then the old man was abruptly silent. Another man nearby, the tall young one with yellow hail spots, began to speak. He motioned to Fargo, then made the gesture of a man pulling at something. Then motions like a fight. Fargo guessed that the Indian was telling the story of his fight with Barney in the graveyard. Sure enough, the brave began to gesture to describe the regiment's arrival and the beating of Fargo. He completed his story. The braves muttered.

"Hello," Fargo said, raising his hand. He would have to try something. The braves fell silent. "I come in peace." He made a gesture like waves. "I am traveling through your land. Let me go on my way." He made a motion like a man walking away into the distance.

The braves watched in silence.

"Why were white men in our place of the dead?" the old man said suddenly. Fargo started.

"You speak English!"

"I understand white man's tongues," the old man said. He paused, waiting for an answer. Fargo thought quickly. It was better not to say too much.

"I was running from other men," Fargo said. "We did not know the way."

"And there was a man with you. A big man. He touched the body of our chief." Fargo thought of Barney pulling the dead Indian off the cairn.

The young warrior interrupted, gesturing wildly in the air. Fargo saw that he was trying to explain something. The old man listened, nodded, and then turned back to Fargo.

"Why did you protect the body of our chief? He was not your chief."

"All men should sleep in peace," Fargo said. The old man grunted and the Indians around him nodded.

"True words," the old man said. "A man who protects the chief's body will go in peace through our lands. You stay here until you can travel. Then your eyes will be covered over and you will go from us. You can have your life."

Fargo nodded. He was lucky. Very lucky. The Indians around him began to get up. The powwow was over. He rose to his feet, as did the old man.

"Thank you," Fargo said quietly. The old man held up his hand as if he did not acknowledge the words.

"My daughters say you are getting stronger every day," the old man said.

"Your . . . daughter . . . daughters?" Fargo asked. "I thought . . . I thought there was only one woman."

The old man laughed. "No. Two. They came into the world together, so they share one face. The laughing one is called White Feather. The shy one is Looks-Down."

"Twins!" Fargo mused. "I thought it was one woman who never sleeps." The old man laughed again, then became suddenly serious.

"Do not stay long," he said.

"No. I will leave as soon as I am strong," Fargo answered.

The old man nodded and climbed the ladder. Fargo followed. He found White Feather waiting for him in the pueblo room.

"You are White Feather," he said, touching a feather on a buckskin parfleche hanging on the wall and pointing to her. She smiled and nodded.

"I am Skye," he said, pointing out to the blue sky.

"Skye," she repeated, nodding. "White . . . Fea
. . . Feather." He smiled and nodded.

The next days were busy as Fargo exercised and ate
and slept, preparing his body for whatever lay ahead.
White Feather attended him during the day and
Looks-Down at night. Both had learned their names
and a few English phrases from him. But there hadn't
been much time to talk with them.

Each night he watched as the moon grew smaller.
Each night he looked out across the canyonlands and
wondered if he would be able to find Antonia, Stalling, and the Silver Maria in time.

Two days later he knew he was strong enough to
leave. He was climbing up and down the ladder easily
now, his muscles aching slightly but healing. His ribs
no longer hurt and the abrasions on his face were
nearly healed.

All afternoon he spent walking vigorously back and
forth on the shelf of the cliff, and lifting rocks to build
up the strength in his arms. He was careful to concen-
trate on his exercises and not to look about too much.
He must not give the impression of being curious
about the location of the pueblo hideout. At dusk he
started to ascend the ladder and heard the old man
call.

"White man!"

He turned and saw the old man approach. He
handed Fargo a skin pouch with a long strap.

"For your journey," the man said. He turned and
left quickly before Skye had a chance to say a word.

He climbed the ladder quickly and, once inside the
room again, opened the pouch. Inside was his empty
Colt revolver, which must have been picked up at the
graveyard, and his knife in the ankle strap. There was
also an animal stomach full of water and many strips
of pemmican. And there were several sticks of fra-

grant bark. Fargo sniffed them. He had heard the Indians chewed bark in the desert to allay thirst. He put all of these back into the skin bag and looked up.

Standing by the entry were White Feather and Looks-Down. He grinned. It was the first time he had seen them together. He pointed to his two eyes and to the two of them, indicating how they were like one eye was to another. They giggled and then looked solemn.

White Feather came forward.

"Skye go," she said, pointing at the skin pouch. He nodded.

"At dawn," he said, making a motion with his hands and fingers like a circle rising from the horizon.

"White Feather . . ." She paused and, lacking the words, waved her hands helplessly in the air and then pulled down the corners of her mouth.

"Skye also," he said, pulling down the corners of his mouth. White Feather reached over to him and removed his fingers, then used her own to make his mouth go upward into a smile. Then she stepped closer, and still holding his hands, placed them on her waist. Fargo looked down at her. She was standing very close to him and he could feel her soft breasts and belly pressing against him. He felt himself harden and as she felt it, she pushed ever so slightly against him.

He glanced up and saw Looks-Down lowering the blanket to cover the entrance. But Looks-Down didn't leave. Instead, she turned and walked toward the blankets on the floor, slipping effortlessly out of her deerskin dress as she moved. Fargo stood with White Feather in his arms and watched as Looks-Down walked splendidly naked toward the blankets on the floor.

8

Fargo watched as Looks-Down stretched herself languidly on the blankets. The red glow of the fire lit the long curves of her body, her lean legs, and narrow hips, the large, dark areolas of her small breasts. She lay there relaxed, as if he were not there, with her legs spread wide, and he saw her dark triangle glistening in the firelight. Where was the shyness, he wondered.

He suddenly realized that White Feather was still in his arms, her hips rubbing rhythmically against his hard readiness. He bent over and kissed her, drinking in her taste like sweet spring sage. She pulled his tongue deeper into her mouth and fumbled with her dress, untying the leather thongs. Suddenly it fell away and he moved his hands over her firm smooth hips, up to cup her breasts with their nipples already crinkled with pleasure. She moaned and guided his hand downward between her legs where he felt the tickle and then the warm wetness of her.

White Feather pulled him gently toward the blankets, not letting their mouths part as they knelt down and then stretched out next to Looks-Down. He reached over and brushed his hand against Looks-Down's thigh. Looks-Down rolled toward them and began to unbutton his shirt and undid his jeans.

He found himself in a tangled mass of smooth woman limbs: a nipple in his mouth, one hand on a breast, the other exploring the hot wetness, someone's mouth on him. Then he felt a tickle and deep tightness around himself. He thrust into it and heard White Feather . . . or was it Looks-Down? . . . moan. He kissed a soft shoulder, a fragrant neck, felt long hair, loosened from a braid, brush his face, his chest, his thighs as he thrust again and again. He felt for the soft breasts, the wet warmth with his fingers, kneading as she panted. Then he shifted, seeking the musk moistness with his mouth, and she cried with surprise. The wet tightness was under him as he thrust again and again, hands and mouth on him, his chest, caressing him, exploring. He felt her tighten and buck under him while he thrust, sucked, and she moaned and then contracted, slipped away from his mouth as he felt the explosion gathering in him and he plunged, tightness again and again, as the firelight shattered into sparks and he shuddered and fell forward onto her, the other wrapped around his neck and his legs entangled. The three of them lay quiet for a while, hardly moving until he felt a soft tickle on his ribs.

"White Feather . . . stop that!" he whispered. The tickling continued. He reached over and found her narrow rib cage. She giggled. He felt another hand . . . hers or her sister's . . . reaching across him, gently caressing and then finding. He heard her gasp—it was Looks-Down—that he was ready again for her. He turned over and kissed Looks-Down deeply and then entered her slowly, her legs coming up to encircle him as he pushed inside her. She gasped. He held back, waiting, cupping her small breasts with his hands, fondling her tight nipples, until she could bear it no longer and gave a cry, clutching at him and tensing. Then he withdrew and quickly rolled over, finding White Feather again, who opened her warmth to him. He was close, close, as he thrust inside her tightness, again, kissing her deeply, the faint sweet smell of sage in her mouth. He ran his hands through her long hair. She came quickly with a shudder and then he let himself, the warm blackness welling up like a welcoming blanket, and he felt himself fall back into it, into their arms, into sleep.

Fargo awoke, aware of the early morning light even with his eyes closed. Beside him he felt warm softness and he remembered the night. He rolled over and his arm grasped nothing but rumpled blankets about him. White Feather and Looks-Down had gone.

He sat up and saw the young brave with the painted hail spots standing inside the door, watching him. It was time to go.

Fargo nodded and rose. He washed, dressed quickly, and slipped the buckskin bag over his shoulder. When Fargo was ready the brave motioned him to the door. Fargo followed down the ladder.

At the bottom another brave stood waiting with a blindfold in his hand. Just then, Fargo sighted two faces at the door of another pueblo, high up. He waved goodbye to White Feather and Looks-Down just as his eyes were covered.

He felt his hand being guided to the shoulder of the Indian who walked ahead of him. The three of them descended the path leaving the Apache hideout. Without the use of his eyes, it was slow going. The Indian walking before him was steady, but even so, it was easy to stumble on the steep rocky trail.

His body was sore but not stiff, the muscles and bones nearly knit. The two weeks of regular food and water had revived him fully and he felt invigorated. His thoughts turned to Stalling.

They walked for several hours, downward, then flat for a long time, then on a rocky trail that seemed to wind through a canyon, though he couldn't be sure. Another flat area, a brief scramble up rocks, and then it seemed they walked in circles for a long time. There was no possibility, he thought, that he would ever find his way back to the ancient pueblos. At last they stopped. He felt two firm hands on his shoulders, pushing him to sit down. He did. He heard the almost silence of their tread diminishing as they walked away from him. He sat and waited for a while, giving them plenty of time to get out of his sight. The Apache had kept their word. They had given him his life. When several minutes had passed, he removed the blindfold and got to his feet.

Before him stretched a plain dotted with creosote and spiny fans of ocatillo. On the horizon he saw the high blue peaks that lay in the direction of the end of the Diablo cutoff. The Apache braves had left him beside the trail. He set off, scanning the ground for any sign of the passing of the regiment. He didn't have far to look. Within a mile he came upon their abandoned campsite.

He knelt down and smelled the charred wood of one of the campfires. An old fire, the pungency gone. More than a week had passed since they camped here, he thought. He scouted about the camp for any other clues. Something white caught his eye beside a rock. He leaned over to retrieve it and recognized the piece of canvas that the Reyes gang had left behind. It had been carefully rolled up and stuffed into a rock crevice. He unrolled it.

The word had been written in charcoal, perhaps with the end of a burned stick. It read Help. Fargo felt a stab of anger and pain. He turned the canvas over, examining it. But that was all there was—the word *help*. Maybe it was all she had time to write. Maybe she could only think of that message to leave behind for someone to find. A message of complete despair. He realized that Antonia would assume that he had died in the graveyard on the mesa.

He rolled up the canvas again and tucked it inside his shirt. If he ever got tired, he thought, the piece of canvas would keep him going.

By nightfall he had reached the end of the Diablo cutoff and the first water hole. The hoofprints of the regiment's mounts left dimples in the sodden bank. Fargo drank from the muddy wallow and refilled the animal stomach flask. He lingered for a while, hoping wild ponies might come to drink.

But the night was silent and soon he turned onto the trail into Yellow Canyon country. He'd never been through this territory, but the track was easy, broad, and rolling across the wide valley bordered by crumbling yellow buttes. As he passed the buttes, he caught glimpses of deep, winding canyons which lay on either side of the valley. He made good time, walking through the night under the waning moon. From time to time he came upon traces of the regiment's passing. Soon, he thought, he would be at the foot of the high peaks in the land known as the heart of the country.

It was midmorning and Fargo was walking close to the base of a gigantic sandstone butte which looked like five fingers when he heard hoofbeats. He immediately took cover behind rocks and kept watch. In a few moments he saw the tall red-haired figure of Major Fox Stalling riding out across the valley. Fargo smiled to see that the major had his right arm bandaged and splinted. He found himself wishing again that his bullet had hit Stalling dead center instead of winging him. Stalling was followed by a half dozen of his men, the Apache scout, and a small figure in men's clothes that could only be Antonia. He wondered where Barney McCann was.

Fargo examined the regiment carefully. They were riding light with no saddlebags. Obviously on a foray. Then where were they camped? The regiment had ridden out of a canyon on the other side of the five-fingered butte. As soon as they were out of sight, he inspected the entrance to the canyon which was framed by pillars of rotten yellow rock. A wisp of smoke rose in the sky. The camp was definitely up in the canyon. There was no one in sight, but he was sure the narrow passageway was under guard.

Fargo returned to the other side of the five-fingered butte and examined the cliffs. Further back was an easy scramble to the top of the ridge. The canyon and the camp lay just on the other side of a low saddle.

"I'll take the high road," Fargo muttered out loud as he climbed up. An hour later he was lying flat on his stomach looking down into the canyon. Below him was the regiment's camp.

Four of Stalling's men lounged about, two playing cards, one whittling, and another stirring something over the fire. Barney McCann was tied to a boulder. Fargo glanced about, taking in the arrangement of the tent and the campfires. They had pitched their camp to the back of the canyon beside a small spring which bubbled up, ran for a short distance, and then disappeared again between rock crevices. The one tent was pitched some distance from where the men had laid the big campfire and their bedrolls and gear.

They had constructed a crude corral at the mouth of the canyon. Stupid, he thought with a smile. Should have put the horses to the rear of the canyon. Men at the entrance. But they had been lazy, wanting to camp as close to the water as possible. Big mistake, Fargo thought.

The floor of the canyon was grassy and dotted with sage and large boulders. Great cover, Fargo said to himself as his eyes traced an easy scramble down the short cliff below him and a series of short dashes from bush to bush to rock to bush, which would bring him within spitting distance—or listening distance—of the camp. At last, at last his luck was turning. He rolled away from the edge of the cliff and found a shady rock overhang. He made himself comfortable, feasted on the Apache pemmican, and drank deeply of the water. He would take a nice, long afternoon sleep. Then he would drop in on Stalling and his troop.

The setting sun splashed red and gold across the feathers of clouds. Purple shadows gathered on the floor of the canyon as Fargo made his way stealthily down the cliff. He took his time, pausing between movements from one rock to the next, watching the quiet camp below. A big cooking fire made a yellow circle in the dusk. Several soldiers busied themselves with chores. The rest of the regiment was still out on their foray.

He was hidden in a stand of sage close to the tent when he heard the hoofbeats of the returning troop. They dismounted at the entrance and left the horses in the corral. Fargo saw Stalling striding toward him, holding Antonia's arm with his good hand, half dragging her along.

"You fucking bitch," he said, throwing her down roughly to the ground beside the tent. "We've spent two goddamn weeks riding all over this hellhole land. Following this scrap of old paper. And no sign of that stupid cave." Fargo saw him pull the map out of his jacket. So, Stalling had gotten the map from Antonia.

The major unfolded it and spread it out on a rock, sitting to study it.

"Williams! Get over here!" Stalling called out. A private hastened toward them. "Translate this again for me, Williams," Stalling said. "And get it right this time."

"Yes. Sir!" Williams removed spectacles from his shirt pocket and put them on. He lit a short candle and held it so that the light fell on the map.

"In the grave, like a snake," Williams read, "go forward and take the left-hand canyon. Past the chimney and the needle's eye. Go for one hour and you have gone almost nowhere. Under the lonely green arms, the Silver Maria waits for the man with a pure heart."

"Going nowhere . . . What the hell is that supposed to mean?" Stalling said. "Why don't they just say where the blasted thing is?"

"Well, Major," Williams said hesitantly. "We did find the deep canyon that winds like a snake. And we found the chimney rock and that needle eye thing last week."

"So what?" Stalling shouted. "For the last seven days we've been riding one hour past that needle and finding absolutely nothing. Go for one hour and you go nowhere. No fucking kidding!"

"I'm sure we can find it soon, Major," Williams said quietly, hoping to calm him down.

"And what's this green arms thing?" Stalling said, as if he hadn't heard Williams. "There's nothing green around that place!" He seized Antonia and hauled her to her feet. Williams backed away and left them alone. "It's your goddamn fault we got into this," Stalling hissed, his face close to hers.

"That's ridiculous," Antonia spat back. "I didn't tell you to take the map from me. I didn't tell you to spend your time looking for some ridiculous treasure that never existed and never will."

"If you didn't believe in the Silver Maria, why did you lie about having the map?" Stalling said. "Why did you hide it until I threatened to finish off that half-wit McCann?" So, Fargo thought. Threatening McCann was how he got Antonia to give him the map.

"Because that map was what my father left me. Even if it is a fake," Antonia said firmly. She had amazing strength, Fargo thought. She was all alone, with no idea that he was alive and might rescue her. And yet, she hadn't lost hope. Or if she had, she had regained it.

It was a good ploy, trying to convince Stalling that the map was a fake. If Stalling couldn't crack the clues, it just might work. It just might. Fox Stalling continued to hold Antonia close to him.

"We'll see," he said. "We'll see." He suddenly pulled her nearer and tried to kiss her, holding her with his good arm. Antonia struggled against him, trying to push him away, but he was too strong. She lifted her hands to his face but he stepped back quickly before she could scratch him and held her at arm's length.

"Hellcat are you?" Stalling said. "I may have only one arm, Antonia Delgado, but I have a dozen men here who can hold you down for me any time I order them to. You're going to give in willingly. Or get it anyway."

"Nunca," she said. "Never!"

"If I can't have the Virgin Mary, then I'm going to have a little Mexican bitch's ass," he said. "Or maybe I'll get both. I didn't slice up your goddamn goody-goody father for nothing."

Antonia spat in his face. Stalling roared, released her arm, balled his fist, and hit her full force across the face. Her head snapped back and she fell to the ground.

Fargo clenched his fists and imagined Stalling's neck

between his hands. He uttered several oaths to himself. Two of the soldiers came running.

"Tie her up for the night," Stalling said. "Tie her tight and dump her in the tent. Where's my supper?" Stalling turned and walked toward the campfire some distance away where the meal was being prepared. Fargo watched as two of the soldiers looked down at Antonia.

"This ain't right," one of them said quietly. Fargo recognized Joe Strayhorn, the blond kid who had picked up Delgado's scarf and had seemed loyal to the murdered colonel. "We gotta do something."

"Yeah?" the other one said. It was Brent Fielding, the tough old soldier Fargo had spoken to on the ride. "Like what? A revolt? That could get us hung. Without a trial. What Stalling says, goes. Orders are orders."

"But, Brent," Strayhorn said. "The major's going crazy. This map thing. And Antonia. Killing that guy in the Indian graveyard. And . . . and what he did to Delgado. I mean, he's the one who ought to be hung."

There was a silence for a moment.

"Yeah," Fielding said quietly. "But who's gonna turn him in?" Fargo noticed another soldier walking quietly up behind Strayhorn and Fielding.

"Well, we could," Strayhorn said excitedly, his voice rising. "We could tie up the major one night. Then we could get all the rest of the guys to go along with us. The major's gone crazy. You know that."

"Oh, yeah?" the third man said, low. The two of them jumped and wheeled about. It sounded like Carmichael, Fargo thought. "Any more talk like that and you'll both hang. Now, move the girl." Carmichael stood and watched as the two men bent over Antonia and tied her up. He checked the ropes.

"Not tight enough," Carmichael said and made

them do it again, pulling them tighter himself before the last knot was tied. "Throw her in," Carmichael said. The two men put her into the tent. Fargo could tell they were being as gentle as possible under the circumstances. "You two have guard duty tonight?"

"Yeah," Fielding said without expression. Fargo felt his hopes rise. Perfect. Fielding and Strayhorn on guard duty. Perfect.

"Well, not anymore," Carmichael said, and Fargo felt his hopes sink. "I don't trust you Mexican-loving bastards. The major's not in the mood to deal with you two tonight. But he will be in the morning when I tell him what I've heard. Get over to the fire and don't move."

The three men made their way to the fire. Fargo sat in thought for a moment. Yes. If everything went as planned, there was just a chance. The troop was gathered around the fire except for the two who guarded the corral and the entrance to the canyon. The regiment was not expecting anyone to drop in, so they weren't guarding the camp at all.

Fargo heard a moan and a rustle from inside the tent. Antonia was stirring. He longed to duck inside and let her know he was here, but there wasn't enough time now. That would have to wait. He had to do other things first.

Skye stole slowly out of the bush toward the scattered bundles of saddlebags, bedrolls, and personal gear that the men had left about on a grassy area, some distance from the fire. Supplies were the first order of business. He kept an ear out toward the campfire as he went about his work.

Fargo hunted for bullets first. He found them and strapped several belts of cartridges around his waist. He never wanted to run out of bullets around Stalling again. Then he lifted a tinderbox and a few candles.

If they found the cave of the Silver Maria, they would need light. If.

Finally, he lifted a few additional guns, stowing them in the Apache bag slung over his shoulder. He started to retreat to the cover of the sage and then thought better of it. He opened several of the packs and removed items, not bothering to see what and deposited them in another bag, some distance away. Then he did the same with several others, placing one man's gear into another's bag. Footsteps came near and he slunk into the shadow of a rock nearby.

". . . in just a minute, when I get my tobacco," the potbellied soldier was saying. Fargo watched as the man approached one of the bags Fargo had just taken supplies from to put in someone else's bag.

"Hey!" the man said to himself, as he searched through his things. "What's going on here? Where's my gun? And my mess kit? What the hell?" His voice brought several others over. "Somebody's been going through my stuff. Pilfering."

The men began to check their own bags.

"Hey, Wilson. Gimme back my pipe. I know you stole it. You always did want it."

"Bullshit, Thomas. I ain't got no pipe of yours. But I can't find my extra bridle in here. The silver one. I bet you took that."

"You calling me a liar?"

"You calling me a thief?"

Fargo watched as the two men squared off, the other men rooting and cheering as they began to swing at one another. The other soldiers, attracted by the noise, gathered around. Some of them also rifled through their bags and found gear missing. Not one of them mentioned the fact that additional items had appeared in their packs. They only seemed to notice what was gone. Complaints and accusations broke out on all sides.

Fargo retreated further. He scanned the camp, looking for Barney. The big man had been tied to a boulder not far from the tent. Good. Now all he had to do was watch the show, wait for the ruckus to die down, and then make off. What he had taken wouldn't be easily noticed and, in the confusion, no one would suspect an interloper had crept into camp.

The voices and sounds of fighting brought Stalling over from the campfire.

"What in the hell is going on here? Sergeant?"

A soldier stepped forward.

"Sir! Gear missing from some of the packs. Sir! Must be a thief in camp."

"What the hell? What's missing?" Stalling roared.

"My pipe," one said.

"My best saddle blanket."

"My canteen."

"My extra bridle."

"If I get my hands on anyone stealing . . ." Stalling began.

"It's probably the Indian," Fargo heard Carmichael say.

"Yeah. Apaches are thieves. Everybody knows that," another added. A murmur of agreement swept the troop.

"That just doesn't make sense," one voice said quietly. Fargo thought he recognized Joe Strayhorn.

"Sure it makes sense," Stalling said roughly. "Where is he?"

"He's still camped by himself over by the corral," one of the men answered.

"Well, string that redskin up in the morning," Stalling said. "From that rock overhang and make it quick. We don't need that lying, stealing son of a bitch any-

139

more anyway. He's served his purpose. String him up and it will save me paying him off. And after that Indian's dead, there'd better not be anything else stolen in this camp."

The men muttered and attended to their bedrolls as Stalling moved off. Some of them finally noticed that their neighbors had items of theirs and some of the exchanges were straightened out. But it was too dark and the men were too tired to make sense of it all.

The troop and Stalling bedded down. The two night guards walked off toward the corral to relieve the evening sentries. In a half an hour all was quiet except for the snoring. Fargo watched as the thin fingernail of moon slipped into view above the lip of the canyon wall. Only a few days more and the Mission Ascension was lost.

He crept quietly to the tent and went in. Antonia lay on her side, turned away from him. He didn't want to scare her or make her cry out.

"It's Skye Fargo," he whispered gently. She started. She was not asleep. He knelt down beside her and hastily untied her bonds. The ropes had cut into her cruelly and her hands and feet had already swollen. She sat up and looked into his face.

"Am I dreaming?" she whispered. Even in the darkness inside the tent, he could see tears rolling down her face, the first time he had seen her cry.

"No," he said, rubbing her hands and feet to get the circulation back. "We're getting out of here. With Barney."

"And the map," she said.

He motioned her to stand and they left the tent. He handed her some of the supplies to carry as they walked quietly toward Barney who was breathing heavily, tied to the boulder. Antonia woke him gently, her hand over his mouth, while Fargo cut the ropes.

When Barney caught sight of Fargo's face he started and a cry of surprise split the silence.

"Shhhh," Antonia whispered in Barney's ear. "Everything will be just fine. Keep quiet and follow us." Barney nodded and they helped him to his feet.

The three of them walked silently, threading their way through the sleeping forms on the ground in order to get beyond the men on the way to the corral. It was dangerous. If any one of the men happened to awaken . . . but it was the only route.

They passed by the form of Major Stalling. Without thinking, Fargo slowly drew the Colt revolver as he looked down at the sleeping major. He couldn't shoot a man in cold blood while he was asleep. Even if he did deserve it. Goddamn it. Fargo was tempted to waken the major and have it out with him at last.

Antonia saw his look and shook her head silently. She was right, of course. They'd have to just make an escape. But he'd get Stalling. Not now, but soon. After they saved the mission.

Antonia knelt down and felt inside the folded jacket that lay on a rock beside Stalling. In a moment she withdrew her hand with a folded paper.

"Iver Maria," Barney said out loud, seeing the map. Antonia and Fargo froze. Antonia raised her hand to her lips and Barney clapped his hand over his own mouth. Stalling stirred and turned over, muttering. After a long moment, they moved on toward the corral.

Fargo smelled the horses ahead and then heard them, the slight stir of sleeping mounts with an occasional snort. He motioned to Antonia and Barney to halt and wait for him. Creeping forward, he scanned the dark corral, a perimeter of sagebrush and some rope lines, with the horses inside tethered together.

Suddenly he saw a yellow flare of light on the other

side of the corral. The guard was lighting a cigarette. He watched and waited. Then he heard the slight crunch of gravel and the second guard walked by him. Fargo followed, walking quietly behind him for a step or two as he drew his Colt and grasped it by the barrel. He brought it down on the back of the man's skull, just hard enough to put him out for a few hours. It was a clean blow and the man dropped like a heavy stone to the earth, moaned once, and then was still.

Fargo stepped away and sighted the red tip of the burning cigarette on the other side of the corral. He made his way quietly around the horses. Several of them smelled him in their sleep and shifted, whinnying nervously. Fargo stopped and waited for them to settle down, keeping his eye on the guard's glowing cigarette.

When the horses had quieted, he sidled along the periphery of the corral until he came up behind the guard. The man stood with his back to Fargo, one foot up on a rock, looking toward the canyon entrance and the moon. Fargo was several paces away from him and closing, his pistol drawn, ready to knock him out.

Without warning, the soldier suddenly threw down his cigarette, stamped on it, and turned.

"Hey!" he yelled. "What's going on here?" His shout disturbed the horses and they stamped and whinnied. The corral was far enough from the camp, almost out of earshot, that it would take more than that to wake the men. A gunshot would do it. Maybe it wouldn't be necessary.

"Keep quiet or I'll shoot," Fargo said quietly, studying him. He was a potbellied man Fargo remembered noticing before. "Get your hands up."

The man did as he was told, his hands shaking.

Fargo cocked the hammer and took slow aim at the man's face. It had a nice effect.

"Look, mister, don't shoot," the man said quietly. "I don't know where you came from, but take some horses if you want. Just leave me alone." The man glanced nervously beyond Fargo, obviously hoping that the other guard would come to his rescue, not realizing the other man was out cold.

"Turn around," Fargo said. "Keep your hands in the air." The soldier did as he was told. Fargo clubbed him and he sank to the ground without a sound. It was going just fine, Fargo thought. Now to fetch Antonia and Barney. Then they would do a little horse stealing.

Fargo turned. The Apache scout stood a yard away, his dark eyes narrowed to slits and focused on Fargo. The dim moonlight glinted on the long blade of the knife he held above his head, ready to lunge.

9

The Apache swiped the air with his knife. The sharp blade whistled through the air. The Indian lunged straight at him. Fargo feinted one direction, then lurched the opposite way, catching the Apache's leg with his boot. The Indian tripped and sprawled face-down, rolling immediately as Fargo threw himself down on top. They rolled over and over, Fargo dodging thrusts of the blade and fighting for a grip on the strong and wiry Indian.

When they stopped, Fargo was looking up into the Apache's face, holding onto the Indian's knife hand which was poised inches above his neck. Skye felt the skin on his throat tingle.

He tightened his grip on the Indian's wrist. The Apache winced as his hand was forced upward, slowly, slowly, the knife wavering in his grasp.

With a final burst of energy, Fargo shook the man's hand and the knife fell. Then he used his powerful shoulder muscles to flip the man over, drove a knee into the Apache's chest, and held him pinioned. The Apache remained tensed, unwilling to give in, his face twisted with rage that he had been beaten.

Fargo looked down at him for a moment, wondering where the Indian's loyalties lay. He had betrayed his tribe by leading the white men. But he hadn't led them to the Apache hideout as Stalling had hoped. At least not yet.

Apaches were renowned as horse stealers. It was said an Apache could spirit away a man's horse right out from under him. The Indian might be useful.

"You understand English?" Fargo asked quietly.

The Apache nodded sullenly.

"Your people saved my life when they found me in the graveyard," Fargo said. "You might say I've got a soft spot for you Apaches right now." The man looked back at him suspiciously, his eyes glittering black.

"So," Fargo continued, "I think you ought to know what I heard in camp tonight. Somebody's been stealing the troop's gear. They think it's you." The Apache opened his mouth to respond, then thought better of it and said nothing.

"Stalling plans to hang you in the morning." This statement had an effect. The Indian squirmed under him.

"You understand the word *hang*?" Fargo asked him. The Apache nodded.

"Stalling said he'd rather hang you than pay you. Understand?" The Indian nodded again. "So, your only chance is to get the hell out of here. Ours, too."

The Apache raised his eyebrows, questioning.

"Yes, ours," Fargo said. "The woman and the big man are over that way. They're coming with me. You've got two choices. You can help us drive all these horses out of the canyon and escape. Or I can put you to sleep like those two sentries. You can take your chances with the regiment in the morning."

The Apache considered the offer for only an instant.

"I help you," he said quickly, the first words he had spoken. Fargo nodded, hoping he could trust the

Apache not to give the alarm. Fargo let him up slowly and then got to his feet. He stooped and retrieved the Indian's knife, handing it over to him, haft first. The Apache took it solemnly, then nodded. Fargo left him, hooked several bridles hanging on a bush, and went to fetch Antonia and Barney.

"Take these," he said, "and get over to the entrance of the canyon. When the horses come walking out, bridle yourself one. They won't be stampeding. I hope."

Fargo returned to the corral and the Apache had disappeared. Damn, he thought. Then he saw the horses stirring slightly. The Indian was among them, moving so slowly and smoothly that the horses made no noise. Fargo began to untie the ropes and move the piles of sagebrush that defined the corral area. He moved very slowly. A herd was easy to spook at night. One false step, the crack of a twig even, might set them off. The camp was just out of earshot, but a stampede would surely awaken the soldiers. If they could spirit the herd away quietly, they would get a good head start.

An opening was made, large enough for the horses to escape toward the canyon entrance. Fargo watched as the Apache bobbed up and down among the rippling backs of the horses, patting their withers and hips, moving them very steadily toward the exit Fargo had made. The first one slipped out and Fargo guided it toward the passageway, slapping it gently on the rear as it passed by. Several more followed, then others, all moving silently and steadily. As the last two passed, the Apache swung up onto one of them, so gracefully that he seemed to be a part of the horse. Fargo followed suit, mounting a muscular bay. They rode in silence, slowly between the dark towering rocks, coming out onto the plain beneath the five-fingered butte.

Antonia and Barney were mounted and waiting. Fargo stopped and retrieved one of the bridles for his mount. The Apache came to a halt beside them.

"Help us drive the horses away from here," Fargo said to the Indian. "Then you can go." The Apache nodded.

Fargo flapped the reins and his bay started forward, frightening several of the horses standing near. They whinnied and began to gallop across the plains. Antonia and Barney rode behind as Fargo and the Indian drove the animals several miles across the wide valley beneath the slender moon.

Fargo felt the powerful animal beneath him. It was a good horse, this bay. Strong, steady, responsive. Still, it was not the faithful Ovaro. The memory of the lost pinto was like a constant thorn piercing his thoughts. Reynaldo Reyes. Goddamn him.

They reined in where the wide valley narrowed and split into several branches. The regiment's horses ran ahead, scattering in all directions. It would take a day at least, Fargo thought, for them to be rounded up.

The Apache sat on his horse a little way away. Fargo held his hand up and the Indian did the same for a moment, then wheeled about and galloped away. In the sky, Fargo saw the first pale light of dawn on the eastern horizon. The sharp point of the moon was sinking in the west.

"We must hurry to find the Silver Maria," Antonia said. "The regiment has found some of the clues. Come, I'll show you."

She led them up one of the valley branches which soon turned into a deep ravine winding back and forth.

"I think this is the grave, like a snake," she called

out. "The left-hand canyon is ahead." Fargo had miscalculated, he realized. He was not prepared for the site of the Silver Maria to be so close to the regiment's camp. He realized that if Stalling suspected that Antonia would head out to find the treasure alone, Stalling might not stop to round up his horses but would march the regiment out on foot. In that case, they might only have several hours until the troop caught up with them. Damn. There hadn't been time to ask her how near they were.

They came to a canyon on the left and turned in. The horses picked their way carefully among the broken rocks of the canyon floor next to a trickling stream. There was no trail and the walls of the canyon were pierced by other arroyos feeding in. Ahead he saw a tall lone rock pillar.

"That's the chimney!" Antonia said excitedly. "And the needle's eye." She pointed to a natural rock bridge arching over a deep cleft. They followed the stream through a thin passage, the horses walking single file, splashing through the stream which ran between the overhanging rock cliffs. On the other side of the narrow pass, Antonia reined in and pulled out the map.

"Now it says—'Go for one hour and you have gone almost nowhere,' " she recited. "Well, the regiment has tried that for a week. Up ahead, the canyon gets smaller and smaller. But they couldn't find anything. Especially any green arms."

Fargo took the map from her and looked at the drawing. It was impossible to make out the small details. He sat and looked about, thinking for a minute. Until you have gone almost nowhere, he thought. Curious words. How was it possible to ride for an hour and go almost nowhere? Unless . . . of course!

He looked back at the narrow passageway they had just ridden through. The monks had hidden the Silver

Maria more than three hundred years before. The canyon had changed in those three centuries, with flash floods and the wearing away of the rocks.

"Stay here," he told Antonia and Barney. He rode back through the passage that the stream had cut through the rocks. But the water might not have cut through when the monks had been here. In that case . . .

On the other side of the passage, he saw the entrance to a narrow canyon. He rode into it for a short ways and, by the light of the brightening dawn sky, saw that the canyon curved sharply toward the right-hand side. He smiled to himself. This was one of those tricky dry canyons that was shaped like a U.

The oxbow canyon had been the streambed long ago. Obviously, the monks had followed the stream until it almost doubled back on itself. After an hour, they were nearly back to where they had been, separated only by a narrow wall of rock. That was the meaning of the words "you have gone almost nowhere."

Since then, the water had cut a new channel, a faster channel, through the rock, which was now the narrow passageway they had ridden through. So, the Silver Maria was not an hour further up the streambed. It was very nearby.

Fargo turned the bay and rode back down the dry canyon, then splashed through the stream again to where Antonia and Barney were waiting.

"It's just up that way," he said, pointing to the canyon which was the other end of the one he had ridden into and which curved left. He explained his reasoning to Antonia and they set off.

"Now, we have to find the green arms," Antonia said. They looked and looked, but it was a parched canyon, full of crumbly rocks and a dry streambed. By midmorning, they had ridden back and forth and still found nothing. Fargo wondered what the regiment was up to.

"Let's halt for a little while," he said. They dismounted and sat in the shadow of a cliff, sharing the Apache pemmican and the water from the flask. He lay back and rested his eyes on the ribbon of blue sky above. The land here was rugged and unforgiving, he thought. He picked out the gray and twisted claw of the stump of a long-dead pine clinging halfway up the side of the cliff. Fargo jumped to his feet.

"The pine tree," he said to Antonia, pointing up.

"The lonely green arms!" she said excitedly. The pine would have been alive and green three hundred years before, clinging alone to the side of the rocks.

Fargo's sharp eyes darted among the jumble of stones and boulders. He climbed over them into a deep defile. He felt a blast of cold air. He followed the waft of coolness and began to roll away the large stones. In a few moments the dark hole of the cave lay before him.

"Come on," he said to Antonia and Barney. "Lead the horses into the ravine and tether them. Then let's go in." The horses were picketed quickly. Fargo had the tinderbox and the supply of candles in his pockets, and they were ready to descend into the cave when Barney began to moan.

"What's the matter?" Antonia asked him, laying her hand on his arm.

"Doan go," Barney muttered. "Inna hole. Doan go."

"It's his fear of being in closed places," Antonia whispered to Fargo. "I noticed it before. Why don't we leave him here to guard the horses?" Fargo nodded. There wasn't much choice. With any luck, they would be back in minutes.

Fargo lowered himself into the darkness, feeling

150

about for a firm footing. About him, the cool wind blew steadily out of the cave. The floor was smooth and he felt his way along the rough wall for a few paces.

Antonia came in behind him. He struck the tinder-box, but the strong winds at the mouth of the cavern blew out the flame.

"We'll have to go forward in the dark," he said. "Feel carefully in front of you with your foot. Follow me."

They slowly made their way along the passage in the windy darkness. Behind them the hole was a ragged patch of white light. Then they turned a corner into impenetrable blackness. Fargo walked forward another pace and the wall fell away from under his hand. The air currents were calmer.

"Let's try a light," he said.

". . . try a light, a light, a light, a light, a light . . ." his voice echoed in the darkness. He struck the tinder-box and lit the candle. He heard Antonia gasp behind him.

They stood at one end of an egg-shaped room with a smooth sloping floor. The rock formation looked as though yellow and orange and rust ruffles were oozing down the walls. The light of the candle danced as the flame flickered and the colored ridges and ripples seemed to be alive.

"*Oh, Dio!*" Antonia whispered. "*Bello*. It's so beautiful." Her whisper echoed in the chamber.

"It is beautiful," he agreed, looking across the room to the two passageways that opened up at the other end. "But which direction do we go?"

They made their way across the space to the openings. Fargo held the candle up to closely examine the entries.

"There," he said. He pointed to an area of the rock

at eye level. Painted on the side of the right-hand entrance was a small red cross. Antonia gasped.

"The mark of the monks!" she said. "The way to the Silver Maria!"

"Exactly," he said. "Let's go."

The passageway descended for a long time, winding back and forth with countless branchings in all directions. At each junction was another of the small red crosses inscribed on the wall to show the way. At each junction, Fargo lifted the burning candle to the wall and let the soot make a large black tail up the rock face.

"This will be easier for us to see on the way out of here," he said. "If we took a wrong turn, we'd never get out."

After a long time the path no longer descended and it became narrower. At times they had to squeeze themselves between the huge rocks. There was complete silence in the tunnel. Then Fargo heard a noise ahead, a slight rustle, like a flapping. He slowed.

They moved cautiously forward as the ceiling lowered and was black and knobby. Fargo lifted the candle to examine the ceiling more closely and just as he realized what he was looking at, the air around them exploded with noise and motion, flapping and high squeaks. Antonia screamed and cowered.

"Duck down," he told her with a laugh. "Bats won't hurt you." In a few moments the tunnel was clear of them. Antonia got to her feet and they continued.

The air grew cooler and moister. Ahead of them, Fargo heard a steady dripping, amplified by echo. The passageway opened up to another room and they saw a huge underground lake, still and glassy. The dim candlelight caught the chalky white rock formations which grew along the shore like rounded fingers pointing up. From the ceiling hung sharp cones of the snowy rock. Fargo held up the candle and looked down into the pale green water. The milky bottom was smooth and rippled. But there was no Silver Maria.

Time was passing. Where was the regiment now? Stalling might suspect that Antonia would come back here to look for the treasure. If he set off on foot, not waiting to round up the horses, the regiment would arrive in another hour or two. Would they ride by Barney, hidden in the defile of the narrow canyon? He began to worry that leaving Barney hadn't been a good decision.

"Let's get on," he said, sighting another red cross on a doorway leading out of the lake room. They hurried through another passage with more branchings. Off to the side, Fargo caught sight of more rooms, red-colored and golden. But they didn't stop to look.

The path began to widen and it was harder and harder to find the mark of the cross among all the passageways. At least, they turned a corner and saw before them a small ornate chamber of dripping orange rock. A rift, a yard wide, cut through the floor, bordered by sharp rock fingers. Fargo held the candle up before him and looked carefully about. Finally, he saw the cross, painted on the wall across the room, next to folded rocks that looked like organ pipes. There was no way around the crevice in front of them, which sliced the room in two. They would have to leap across it, he realized. He inched to the brink of the gap and looked down. Below was pitch black. He could not see the bottom.

"Think you can jump this?" he asked Antonia. She nodded. "I'll go first and hold my hand out for you."

He leapt easily across the dark chasm, then turned to help her. She made the jump easily enough, but then she faltered as she landed and stumbled back toward the crevasse. He grasped her arm and pulled her toward him as she knocked several stones into the darkness.

"Mierde!" she said. After a moment he heard a sound from below echoing up the abyss. Like something falling into water.

"What was that?" Antonia whispered. Fargo realized that the stones she had knocked in had taken a long time to fall. He grasped a handful of pebbles and tossed them over the edge. He waited. Several long seconds later, he heard the sound again.

"There's another lake way down there," he said. "Way down."

They walked toward the cross on the wall. The folded golden rocks were full of crannies which revealed themselves as they neared. Just as a large opening came into view, Fargo held his candle high and Antonia gasped.

"Oh, Dio!" she muttered, crossing herself. The light caught the stiff form of a slender woman in heavy folded robes. The statue stood on a natural rock pedestal. One hand was raised as if she were blessing someone. The edge of her carved robe was a wide band of encrusted jewels. Fargo and Antonia drew nearer.

The Maria's serene face was beautifully carved. The light danced on the embedded jewels—golden, purple, red, blue, green. Antonia put her hand out to touch the Silver Maria, as if to make it real, tracing the edges of the colored gems.

"At last," she said. "The Silver Maria. We can save the mission. And all of the children. She belongs to them."

Fargo leaned down and hoisted the Silver Maria in his arms. The figure was the size of a small child, but very heavy and awkward. They had gone several steps toward the crevasse when Fargo heard a distant sound, almost beyond the limit of hearing.

"Sh," he said.

It came again, echoing and far away. Was he hearing something or not? Barney calling? He wasn't sure. It was hard to hear in the echoing room.

"I'll just be a few minutes," he said, putting the statue down. He would have to back up the tunnel a little in order to hear more clearly. He slid the knife out of his ankle holster and handed it to her along with an extra candle. "Just in case," he said.

He leapt across the abyss again and retraced the way, hurrying along. For a while he heard nothing. When he reached the lake room, he heard it again. A distant boom. Then voices. More than one. It could only be the regiment. Damn. And, just in case they didn't notice the red crosses, he had left them very clear smoke marks on the wall marking which way he and Antonia had gone. The regiment would have no trouble following them.

Just then, a high-pitched scream pierced the air and echoed.

"Antonia!" he said out loud, running back to find her.

When he entered the room, he saw her, one hand grasping a rock finger as she dangled into the abyss. Beside her, on the brink of the chasm, lay the Silver Maria. In an instant, he realized she had been dragging the statue across the room and had slipped on the slick rock. As he leapt across the chasm, her hand slipped on the rock.

"Hold on!" he called. He stuck the candle into the floor and, throwing himself down on the edge of the cliff, reached out to grasp her just as her grip failed. He held her by the wrist, suspended above the pitch blackness below.

He began to lift her straight up out of the chasm and she reached up with her other hand to get a hold. She grasped the Maria which teetered and then rocked off the edge. Fargo made a grab for it and clutched at the smooth silver hand of the statue. With one hand he held Antonia and with the other, the Silver Maria. Just then the candle sputtered and failed. It was completely dark.

Fargo swore. He felt his body slide toward the edge, pulled by the weight of Antonia and the silver statue. He dug his boots into the rock. In another moment, all three of them would plunge into the chasm. His palms were sweating and he felt the smooth silver statue slipping from his grasp.

"I can't save you both," he said to Antonia between clenched teeth. There was nothing else to do. He let go.

He steadied himself on the cliff with his now free hand, took a deep breath and pulled Antonia to safety, dragging her onto the ledge. Below, he heard the echo of the statue plunging into the dark lake so far beneath them. The Silver Maria was lost forever.

"Goddamn it," he muttered. In the darkness he heard Antonia trying to catch her breath. He pulled out the tinderbox and relit the candle. He heard the voices again. Nearer now.

"The regiment," he said.

There was no time to lose. He hauled Antonia to her feet and they leapt again over the abyss. She was still panting with fright.

"About the Silver Maria . . ." she gasped between breaths.

"Later," he said.

He led, hurriedly retracing their steps, following the crosses and his soot marks back toward the entrance.

He would have to mislead the soldiers, he realized, if they were going to get out of this cave alive.

They hurried through the lake room again, then squeezed through the passageway where the bats had been. They ran up the ascending hall with the branchings on all sides. The voices were much louder ahead of them but, because of the echo, it was impossible to judge the distance. They could come around the corner at any moment, Fargo thought. He stopped and made a soot mark on one of the branchings. Then made another mark which obscured the red cross. That would confuse them.

"This way," he whispered to her. They ran down a narrow passageway and again he stopped, making another soot mark to mislead the soldiers.

"Stay here," he said, pushing her into a crevice behind a rock pillar. He left her in the dark and ran a short way down the tunnel and made more marks. Then he lit another candle, since his was burning low, and set the short one into a niche in the wall. He returned to Antonia and pressed himself behind the pillar beside her. He blew out his candle. The darkness wrapped around them and he felt her huddle near.

The voices came closer, but it was hard to distinguish the words because of the echo.

"There's another!" he heard someone call out distinctly. "And another!"

There was a silence and Fargo smiled to himself. They must be at the branching where he had left several marks, he thought. There seemed to be some heated discussion, though he couldn't make out the words. They were probably breaking up into search parties. Then voices came nearer. He peered around the corner and saw a dim light flickering. In a moment some of the soldiers passed so close by he could have reached out and touched them. They halted and Fargo stilled his breath, feeling Antonia stiffen beside him.

"Hey, Sarge," one of them whispered. "I see light up ahead. Think she found the treasure?"

"Get your guns out," said Carmichael's voice. "There were three horses with Barney McCann, so she's not alone. But who the hell is she with?"

"Maybe somebody deserted during the night," another voice said. "And we miscounted."

"Yeah? Well, he's gonna get the same reward as Fielding and Strayhorn did this morning," hissed Carmichael. "The major's got a shot in the back for any man caught deserting."

"Or even thinking about it," said another under his breath.

"Remember our orders," Carmichael said. "The major said to shoot the bitch. C'mon."

Fargo felt Antonia tremble beside him. The soldiers moved on toward the candle. Fargo waited a moment and then, pulling Antonia behind him, slipped out into the main tunnel and felt his way back up the path toward the entrance. They moved in the dark at first. Then as the voices grew dimmer behind him, he lit a candle and they raced up the tunnel. The passage wound upward and at last they came to the orange room and the final tunnel. As the brightness of the entrance came into view, Fargo drew his Colt and walked slowly forward. Behind him, he heard the voices again. Some of the soldiers were heading back toward the entrance.

He waited until his eyes adjusted to the glaring white light outside. Then he slowly poked his head through the hole.

Barney McCann sat on a rock, looking down, his hands tied behind him. There didn't seem to be anyone else around. Fargo ventured to put his head and shoulders out of the entrance. No one in sight. Barney looked up and saw him.

McCann stood excitedly and began moaning, trying to gesture with his shoulders. Fargo eased himself out of the entrance and walked a pace or two toward Barney. He heard Antonia following.

"Drop it," he heard Stalling say behind him, accompanied by the unmistakable click of a gun. In a flash Fargo realized Stalling had sent his men inside the cave while he sat waiting above the cave entrance.

Fargo grabbed Antonia and dove to one side and turned, drew, fired, and caught Stalling in the leg. The major screamed and a bullet grazed Fargo's thigh. The shots resounded through the narrow defile. Fargo heard the sound of loose rock shifting up above as he took cover, pushing Antonia ahead of him.

Fargo popped up, but the major had taken cover. Barney sat on the rock, cowering.

"I thought you were dead, Fargo," the major shouted. He sounded pissed. Real pissed.

"I've come back," Skye answered. "Unfinished business." He glanced up at the rocks for a route to sneak up on the major. Everything was exposed. No way.

"Give up, Fargo," Stalling called out. "My men will be out here in another minute. You're outnumbered."

"When they come out of that hole, I'll pick 'em off one by one like jackrabbits," Fargo said.

There was a silence. The major didn't like that either.

"And I'll pick off Mr. McCann," said Stalling. A bullet zinged and ricocheted off a rock beside Barney. Fargo heard the rocks shift above them again. At the sound of the gunfire, Barney looked up toward where the major was hidden and slowly rose to his full height.

"Give up, Fargo," Stalling said, "or the next one goes dead center." Fargo popped up again, sighted the side of the major's head, with its tuft of red hair, and squeezed off a shot. The major screamed.

"Get down, Barney!" Fargo shouted. But the big man didn't seem to hear. He began to walk toward where Stalling was hidden.

"My ear! Son of a bitch!" Stalling shrieked. The major rose, blood running down the side of his face, and shot at McCann, advancing on him. Barney jerked at the impact of the bullet, faltered, and then continued to walk straight toward Stalling.

"No!" Antonia screamed. Fargo shot again, but the major ducked. Barney continued forward. Again, Stalling rose and shot McCann at close range. Barney staggered forward, then with a final burst of fury he threw himself onto Major Stalling.

"Delgado! Delgado! Delgado!' McCann shouted. The word was loud and clear as he hit the major. They rolled to the ground as the major pumped three more bullets into McCann. The sound of the gunfire resounded up the defile. Fargo heard a loud crack above them and the rumble of boulders coming loose. The sound had loosened the crumbly rock.

A boulder crashed down and shattered, spraying rock chips, and rocks were bouncing down the hillside, falling around them. Fargo glanced up and saw a massive sheet of rock begin to slide off the face of the cliff.

"Run!" he shouted, pulling Antonia along behind him out of the defile. At the entrance he loosened the tethers of the three horses and they followed. Behind him he heard a piercing scream. It was Stalling, he realized, trapped beneath McCann's body and struggling to free himself.

Fargo and Antonia dodged the falling stones and stumbled out into the wide canyon. They ran clear of the avalanche and then turned to look. The cliff above was dissolving as layers of rock slid down into the ravine, like a massive gray waterfall. A roaring filled the canyon, the bellow and crash of boulders smashing, splintering, shattering. The brown dust rose in a cloud, enveloping them.

They coughed and watched as the avalanche slowed, then stopped. A rock bounced down the hillside. Then all was still. Above them was the new cliff face. Below, the ravine was now a huge pile of broken rock. Barney, Major Stalling, the regiment, and the entrance to the cave, were buried forever.

Fargo saw the tears on Antonia's cheeks.

"Barney McCann was a loyal friend," she said, crossing herself. They stood in silence for a long moment, then turned away.

"I'm sorry about the Silver Maria," Fargo said. "Maybe we can find some other way to save the mission." But he knew, as he spoke, that with only one more day to go, it was hopeless.

"I'm not sorry," Antonia said, smiles in her eyes. She drew Fargo's knife from her belt, which he had given her in the cave, and handed it back to him. "This was most useful," she said. She put her hands deep into her pockets and brought up handfuls of jewels which glittered and shone in the afternoon sunlight. "I used it to pry these loose while you were investigating the noise," she said. "It's more than enough to save the mission and pay your fee."

He grinned.

"Let's ride," he said. As he leapt onto the bay, he thought again of his pinto.

An hour later they rode into the town of Lealtad, a dusty huddle of abode hovels. They dismounted at the trading post and went inside.

The fat proprietor bustled forward.

"Forasteros," he muttered to them.

"Sí," Antonia answered, removing her hat and letting her long hair fall down around her shoulders. "We are strangers here." The man took in the sight of Antónia in her men's clothes.

"Señor, I would hide this woman if I were you," the man said quietly. "Reynaldo Reyes is in town. No woman is safe."

Fargo grinned. What luck.

"Reyes, eh? I'm an old friend of his," Fargo said. The shopkeeper started, fear flitting across his face as he looked from Fargo to Antonia and back again. "Where is Reyes now?"

"By the corral," the proprietor said. "Betting on horses and looking for women."

"I'm coming with you," Antonia said firmly, starting to put her hair back up under her hat. Fargo glanced quickly over the paltry supplies of the store and pointed to two brightly colored serapes and sombreros. He and Antonia donned them quickly and left the trading post.

Once out on the dusty street, they followed the sound of men shouting and laughing and soon saw the Reyes gang gathered around a corral. The men were lounging around the fence laughing and drinking. As Fargo and Antonia approached, one man drew his pistol and rested it on the fence. He took aim and shot. The bullet kicked up a fan of dust at the feet of a horse galloping around and around inside the corral. The horse didn't recoil, but ran on. It was the black-and-white Ovaro.

Fargo drew near to Reyes, who was watching the pinto.

"Some horse," Fargo said casually. Reyes looked over at him, taking in his and Antonia's *vaquero*

162

clothes in a glance. Skye hoped they wouldn't be recognized.

"*Sí,*" said Reyes. "A magnificent horse. But no one can ride it."

"I've never met a horse I couldn't ride," Fargo said.

Reyes laughed and several of the men nearby whooped.

"Not this horse, señor. This pinto is completely wild. She has bucked every man who has tried."

Fargo looked out again at the Ovaro. It had been mistreated, he could see—not enough food and its coat was dusty. But the strength still flowed in its powerful legs and chest, the old fire shone in its eyes.

"I can ride that horse easily," said Fargo nonchalantly. Reyes laughed.

"Would you like to bet?" he said. The gang whooped.

"Sure," Fargo said.

"But what do you have to bet?" Reyes said, his eyes glittering.

"How about the Silver Maria?"

Reyes laughed again, doubling over.

"Ha! The Silver Maria. This is ridiculous."

Fargo nodded to Antonia and she pulled the map out of her pocket, unfolded it, and waved it before Reyes. The bandit made a grab for it, but she snatched it out of his grasp.

"This looks very old, it is true," Reyes said, eyeing the map which Antonia held just out of reach. Reyes was not a stupid man and Fargo saw the greed glitter in his eyes as he looked at the map.

"What do I get if I win?" said Fargo.

"You will not win. But name your price."

"The wild horse."

"Done," said Reyes, chuckling. "This is the most fun I've had in a long time."

Fargo climbed over the fence and approached the pinto. It smelled him, recognized him at once, and grew quiet. He leapt onto its back.

"Que passa?" Reyes shouted, furious. "What is going on?" He drew his carved silver revolver.

Fargo and the Ovaro sailed over the fence. Skye leaned down and scooped Antonia up, setting her in front of him. They galloped up the street.

"Duck down," he said, hunching over her as the shots zinged around them. He glanced back. The Reyes gang was mounting their horses. They would give chase. He thought quickly.

"Give me the map!" he said to Antonia. She fumbled for it and pressed it into his hand. He turned around again and saw the Reyes gang riding in pursuit, Reynaldo in the lead. Fargo waved the map over his head. Then he let go of it and turned to watch as it fluttered to the ground.

Reyes reined in and dismounted to retrieve the map. The gang came to a stop and huddled about.

"That will keep them busy for quite a while," said Fargo, imagining the Reyes gang spending weeks hunting for the lost entrance to the cave.

Antonia laughed. Fargo patted the strong neck of the Ovaro beneath him, the faithful horse which had been with him for so long. The pinto was fast. There was just enough time to ride to the Mission Ascension before the new moon rose. And after that, there would be time for other things, he thought, as he tightened his arms around Antonia.

LOOKING FORWARD!

**The following is the opening
section from the next novel in the exciting
Trailsman series from Signet:**

THE TRAILSMAN #130
MONTANA FIRE SMOKE

*1860, the Montana Territory north
of Medicine Rocks, a tinderbox
land waiting to ignite. . . .*

Trouble

Just over the top of the ridge.

If not trouble, something. The ears told him. Not his ears, the tall, black-furred ears of the magnificent Ovaro he rode. They were flicking forward, then back, turning sideways then forward again. Those ears always told him when there was something he hadn't picked up, even with his own wild-creature hearing. Skye Fargo moved the horse forward and carefully crested the ridge to look down a short slope thick with fescue grasses and wiry brush. He instantly saw the figure near the bottom, a girl, half running and half falling down the other side of the slope.

Indian, he thought when he saw the jet black hair and slender shape under the deerskin dress. Northern

Cheyenne. Every tribe had its distinctive way of cutting women's garments, and this dress had the rounded contours of the upper sleeves and the straight line across the garment that marked the Cheyenne style. Skye Fargo's lake blue eyes narrowed as he sat motionless atop the Ovaro with its black fore- and hindquarters and pure white midsection gleaming in the afternoon sun. The young woman was plainly running in fear, and he was wondering why when the three U.S. Cavalry troopers rode into sight on their dark bay army mounts. One immediately sent his horse down the opposite slope toward the girl, while the other two rode to the end of the slope to cut her off.

The Cheyenne girl, who was almost at the bottom of the slope, continued running toward the small ravine. She started to turn to the right, saw the one trooper coming fast at her, and spun the other way. Her ankle turned under her and she gave a short cry of pain as she fell and rolled to the bottom of the slope. She rose, started to run, but with a limp now, and the first trooper, sergeant's insignia on the sleeve of his blue uniform, was upon her. He reached down to catch her, but she managed to spin away from him. She limped in the other direction, only to see the other two troopers blocking her way. She tried to climb up the slope but this time the sergeant brought his horse around to strike her a glancing blow.

She sprawled forward and the other two troopers came up and Fargo watched all three leap from their horses. The sergeant, a beefy-faced man with a stocky build, reached her first and flung her to the ground. She landed on her back and he leaped onto her at once. The girl twisted and Fargo saw her bring her leg up to knee her attacker, but the man twisted and she struck only the side of his thigh. "Try again, squaw bitch," the trooper laughed and pressed her back again on the ground where she still struggled in fury. "Get over here and hold her damn arms," the sergeant yelled and the other two hurried over to take the girl's arms and pull them up over her head. The beefy-faced sergeant pushed the deerskin garment upward and Fargo caught the flash of lithe, coppery-skinned legs.

He knew but one thing. What was taking place before him was contrary to all army regulations, to say nothing of human decency. But he wasn't about to go shooting at U.S. Cavalry troopers without knowing a lot more than he did. That could get a man into a lot of trouble. The beefy-faced one atop the girl and the other two all looked up as Fargo came down the slope. "That'll be enough, Sergeant," Fargo said quietly as he reined to a halt.

The man didn't move. Neither did the two troopers holding the girl's arms. Fargo glanced at the girl and saw the uncertain pleading in her jet black eyes. "Keep riding and fast, mister," the sergeant snarled from atop the young woman. "This is army business."

"No shit. Looks sort of personal to me," the big man atop the pinto commented.

"We're interrogating her," the sergeant snapped.

"What page would that be in the army manual?" Fargo asked blandly.

"My page, smart-ass," the man said, his beefy face growing redder. "You riding or do we take care of you, too?"

"I'll be more trouble. Guaranteed," Fargo said.

"Get his ass," the sergeant barked to his two men. "I'll keep hold of her."

The other two let go of the girl's arms and bounded to their feet. One was thin and tall, the other medium height, and Fargo watched them come toward him. They separated in order to rush him from both sides without picking up their rifles, he noted. They didn't want shooting for their own reasons and he didn't want any for his, not till he knew more. He waited atop the Ovaro, and at a grunt from the tall one, both rushed at him from different sides. Fargo dug heels into the Ovaro's sides and the horse reared and the two troopers automatically ducked away. The Ovaro came down hard on its powerful forelegs, and at another touch from Fargo, it swung its rump around and the tall trooper flew a half-dozen feet through the air. Fargo leaped from the saddle and saw the other one coming at him from around the rear of the horse.

He held a knife in his right hand, a standard, army-issue all-purpose bivouac knife, and Fargo, knees bent and arms hanging loosely, let the man lunge. He measured split seconds and twisted his upper body six inches to the right as the man struck. He felt the knife blade whistle past his ear, and then he was bringing his hand up, closing an iron grip around the man's arm. He twisted, brought his other arm across, and the trooper went spinning. Fargo dropped low and threw a right into the man's midsection, and the soldier dropped to one knee with a grunt. Fargo's kick sent the knife flying from his hand. He dived for the knife as it skittered away, but Fargo quickly grabbed the man by the shoulder and spun him around.

A short left hook split the skin on his cheekbone. He staggered, and a short, driving right cross smashed into his face. His nose erupted claret as his eyes crossed and he went down. Fargo turned in time to see the tall trooper rushing at him, and he backed away. With a quick glance he saw the sergeant still holding the girl down, still straddling her, but the soldier was watching the fight taking place alongside him. Fargo ducked under two long-armed punches the tall trooper threw, trying to use his reach advantage. Fargo feinted and the man let go with two more long blows, thrown from too far back with little power left in them, and Fargo blocked them easily. He backed again, then again, and the trooper came after him, growing stupidly bold. He swung again and Fargo ducked, but this time his left shot out and smashed into the side of the man's jaw. The trooper grunted, staggered sideways, and Fargo's looping right was instant, slamming into the man's eye.

The tall, thin form went down with blood streaming from a gash over his eye, and Fargo saw the beefy-faced sergeant push up from the girl and rush forward. "Goddamn," the man snarled and drew the gun from its holster, a standard-issue Army holster-pistol, a six-shot, single-action weapon. But the man held it by the rounded barrel to use the long, heavy butt as a club. He still wanted no shots, it was obvious. He roared, catapulted his thickset body forward, and brought the gun butt down in an arc. Fargo drew back his head to avoid the blow, then twisted aside as the man's charge carried him forward. He stuck a foot out to trip the man, and the soldier stumbled but avoided falling. Fargo tried to wrap an arm around the sergeant's neck but had to fling himself backward as the man sent the gun butt in a flat arc. The man was quicker than he expected, Fargo realized, and he had to duck away from another fast, short blow that grazed his shoulder.

"Fucking busybody," he heard the man mutter as another chopping blow of the gun butt came at him. This time he swung a short left that hit into the man's ribs, and the trooper winced as he swung the gun butt again, upward this time, and Fargo barely avoided the blow as it grazed his jaw. The blow had left the man off balance, and Fargo lifted a tremendous, looping right that caught the soldier on the point of his chin. The trooper staggered, somehow avoided going down, and tried to bring the gun butt up again, but now his arm movement was slow. Fargo's blow crossed over the man's arm and landed flush in the center of his face. The beefy face grew red as a dozen little blood vessels broke and the thickset figure collapsed. He half sat, half lay on the grass, shaking his head, the gun on the ground now.

Fargo kicked it aside as he strode past, his eyes sweeping the small ravine for the Indian girl. She had run off—limped off—he corrected himself, as he swung onto the Ovaro. Instantly he picked up the marks of her trail in the tall brush and followed where she'd bent back young growths as she hurried forward. The brush ended at another downward slope of land that broke off into gullies on all sides, but her prints were fresh and clear. He caught up to her as she neared a small brook. She turned as she heard him approach, shrank back against a mound of earth, and picked up a rock in one hand.

He slowed to a halt and swung down from the saddle to see fear, defiance, and uncertainty all shouldering each other in her face. A handsome face, even-featured with an unusually delicate nose and wide-spaced eyes, well-fleshed lips, and good, high cheek-bones to carry it all off. Definitely Cheyenne, he told himself, in her height and her features. The majority of the tribes were only forty-five to seventy percent full-blooded, someone had found in a survey, but the Cheyenne, Wichita, and Arapaho were some ninety percent full-blooded.

"I won't hurt you," he said, using sign language to emphasize his words. The Cheyenne used the Algon-quian tongue, and Fargo spoke enough of it to get along, though not so well as he did the Siouan lan-guage. She blinked but he saw her visibly relax. She straightened up and stepped toward him. He motioned to the rock in her hand and she dropped it. High, round breasts were thrusting forward even under the deerskin dress.

"You save me from your own bluecoats," she said questioningly.

"They were doing wrong," he said.

"Your people," she said with cold disdain, the black eyes finding icy fire.

"Are there not Cheyenne who do wrong?" he asked and she took in his answer without showing anything in her handsome face. "Why did they chase you?" he questioned.

"They saw me," she said, telling him that was rea-son enough. "There were three of us. We ran in dif-ferent ways."

"All beautiful squaws?" he pressed.

"Two old women. We were digging camas root. We went too far." She took a step and he saw her wince at the pain in her ankle. It had begun to swell and lose its slenderness. He stepped back and swung onto the Ovaro and held out one hand.

"Come. You can ride with me," he said. She searched his face for a long moment and then stepped to the horse, ignoring the pain of her ankle. There was a decidedly regal bearing to her. Any fear she had was wrapped in quiet strength. But this was not unusual for a Cheyenne, he knew. He helped her swing onto the horse and she chose to sit behind him in the saddle. He smelled fresh lemon oil on her, the scent quietly provocative. She pointed south and he followed a gully to where it widened into a gently hilly plain. She rode in silence, not touching his back, and when he reached a stand of cottonwoods her hand pressed his elbow and he halted. She let him help her swing down from the horse and he dismounted with her.

"They would have killed me, your bluecoats," she said softly, and he saw no gain in denying what was probably the truth.

"They are not *my* bluecoats," he said.

Her eyes stayed on his, round and black and grave. She put her hands together in a sign of gratitude. "You are good," she said simply.

"And you are very beautiful," he smiled. "What do your people call you?"

"Red Flower," she said and waited.

"Fargo . . . Skye Fargo," he said. "Some call me the one who makes trails . . . The Trailsman." She took in his answer and nodded slowly. "I can take you further," he offered.

"No," she said and he smiled, understanding that trust would go only so far.

"Red Flower will remember," she said, and he understood her meaning. She was in his debt and he watched her turn and walk into the cottonwoods, tall and straight, allowing only a slight concession to the sore ankle. When she vanished in the trees he climbed back into the saddle and rode back at a fast canter. He wasn't surprised when he reached the small ravine below the ridge. The three troopers were gone and he spat to one side as he sent the Ovaro up to the top of the ridge line. The army was made up mostly of good, dedicated men, decent and honorable men. But it had its share of misfits, especially out here where they sent the bottom of the barrel.

Still, these three hadn't been riding out here in this country alone. He halted at the end of the ridge and scanned the land that spread out below; there were rolling hills and good tree cover but plenty of open land. This was fertile land, rich enough to offer food, clothing, and shelter to last through the harsh winters. Land of the mountains—Montana, the early Spanish explorers had named it, and aptly enough, for to the west the towering Rockies reached up to touch the sky. He had seen small game all over as he'd ridden, plus plenty of bear and elk, weasel and marten, and in the crystal clear lakes, pike and muskellunge bigger than a fat beaver. He had come off a trail drive up from south Wyoming and was close enough to visit Betty Harrison. She had come out here with a husband who got himself killed trying to saddlebreak a sunfisher. But she'd stayed on, hired some hands, and made a go of a small ranch. Fargo smiled as he thought about Betty Harrison. He'd known her back in Kansas, before she thought of marrying.

Full-bosomed, always a tad on the heavy side, Betty was every bit as willing and eager as she'd ever been when he appeared at the ranch. Maybe more so, he murmured silently, and they had turned the clock back together, a clock made of pillowy breasts and large, soft lips, of hips wide and full and made for riding. There'd never been any false modesty about Betty Harrison and there still wasn't and the visit had been all any man could want. When he left, he decided to circle north. It had been a good while since he'd ridden the north Montana territory and, like Betty Harrison, it hadn't changed much.

It was still a land that with the snap of a finger could take your breath away with its beauty and your life away with its danger. That had been reaffirmed in the flame-tipped beauty of the wild columbine and the burned-out Conestogas he had passed, in the red-purple brilliance of the blazing star and the arrows imbedded in charred cabins. It was still a land where calm was but a thin veil over fury. His reflections snapped off as he spotted the sign he had been seeking—a thin column of dust in the distance. He watched the column head east, spurred the Ovaro from the ridge, and let the horse out into a full gallop when he reached the rolling terrain below. The line of dust grew more distinct as he closed distance, and he slowed to a halt when the dust turned into a column of U.S. Cavalry in their blue-and-gold uniforms.

He counted sixteen troopers with one officer riding lead at the head of the column, and he waited as they rode up to a halt. "Afternoon," Fargo said pleasantly as his eyes swept over the column. He didn't have to look beyond the three troopers who were directly behind the officer. The tall, thin one wore a bandage over his right eye, the one beside him a patch on his split cheek and another on his nose. The sergeant's face was swollen and bruised, his lips thickened and puffy.

"Captain Burton Cogswell," the officer said, and Fargo saw imperiousness in a face too young to have earned it. The man's very crisp manner marked an eastern officers' school, most likely West Point. "You been riding alone through here?" the captain asked, and Fargo nodded. "See any Cheyenne?" Cogswell asked.

"Nope," Fargo said blandly.

"Three of my men I sent ahead as scouts were attacked," the captain said. "They were ambushed by six of the damn savages."

Fargo let his eyes move slowly across the three troopers. "Six?" he remarked and saw each of the three men avoid his eyes. "How come they were beat on instead of just killed?" he asked the captain.

"The Cheyenne obviously wanted to take prisoners," Cogswell said with a trace of impatience. "Apparently you don't know the Indian, mister."

"I know the Indian a damn sight better than you do, I'd wager," Fargo said, letting a smile take the edge off his words. Captain Burton Cogswell fastened him with a stony stare.

"What's your name, mister? And how do you know the Indian so well?" he pushed forward.

"Fargo . . . Skye Fargo. Some call me the Trailsman. You can ask General Leeds about me. He still commander in the territory?" Fargo asked.

"Yes, but he works out of Fort Ellis," Cogswell said and Fargo smiled inwardly. The mention of General Leeds had made the captain draw back some. "How do you come to know the general?" Cogswell queried.

"Did some special assignments for him," Fargo answered.

"We're operating out of a small field post near Desmond Kray's trading post. There's half a town there called Postville. You know Kray?" the captain asked.

"Never met him."

"We're riding back to the post. You're welcome to ride along with us if you've a mind for your scalp," Cogswell said.

"You having troubles?" Fargo questioned as he swung the Ovaro alongside the captain's mount.

"I'm trying to keep some discipline around here," Cogswell said. The imperiousness was quick to return to his voice, Fargo noted. "Authority and force, that's what these damn Cheyennes understand," Cogswell said.

"I know the northern Cheyenne. Disciplining them could be walking a tightrope," Fargo suggested.

"No tightrope for me," the captain bristled. "There are a number of settlers now in this region and they look to the army for protection. I intend to see that they get it."

He waved the column forward and Fargo's glance went to the sergeant and the two other battered troopers. Their cut and swollen faces didn't hide the nervous apprehension in their eyes. Fargo decided to remain silent, for now, anyway. If the captain was facing real trouble with the Cheyenne he'd need every body and gun in his command.